A Tycoon Too Wild to Wed

CAITLIN CREWS

HARLEQUIN
PRESENTS

HARLEQUIN®
PRESENTS™

Recycling programs
for this product may
not exist in your area.

ISBN-13: 978-1-335-59336-8

A Tycoon Too Wild to Wed

Copyright © 2024 by Caitlin Crews

For questions and comments about the quality of this book,
please contact us at CustomerService@Harlequin.com.

TM and ® are trademarks of Harlequin Enterprises ULC.

Harlequin Enterprises ULC
22 Adelaide St. West, 41st Floor
Toronto, Ontario M5H 4E3, Canada
www.Harlequin.com

Printed in Lithuania

MIX
Paper | Supporting
responsible forestry
FSC® C021394

Brita couldn't seem to look away from the man before her, who hadn't moved from the threshold, yet still seemed to crowd the rambling kitchen.

Until everything was airless.

Particularly her.

He was so *severe*, she thought. Not one to be trifled with.

All he did was stand there, and though the way he held his body should have seemed nonchalant, it wasn't.

Nothing about him is casual, she found herself thinking, the way she would about any wild thing, and no matter that this one wore a dark suit that whispered of wealth and consequence instead of a pelt or some fur.

There was an intensity that rippled within him, and from him.

He gazed at Maria for a long moment, acknowledging her, and then he shifted that gaze to Brita. And held it there.

Lightning struck again, hard and deep.

"I'm not here for the family," he said, and the way he looked at her, Brita thought he knew. She thought he knew every crackle of that lightning that struck her again and again, every kiss of electricity and wonder. "I'm here for you."

USA TODAY bestselling, RITA® Award—nominated and critically acclaimed author **Caitlin Crews** has written more than one hundred and thirty books and counting. She has a master's and PhD in English literature, thinks everyone should read more category romance and is always available to discuss her beloved alpha heroes—just ask. She lives in the Pacific Northwest with her comic book—artist husband, is always planning her next trip and will never, ever read all the books in her to-be-read pile. Thank goodness.

Books by Caitlin Crews

Harlequin Presents

Willed to Wed Him
A Secret Heir to Secure His Throne
What Her Sicilian Husband Desires
A Billion-Dollar Heir for Christmas
Wedding Night in the King's Bed

Innocent Stolen Brides

The Desert King's Kidnapped Virgin
The Spaniard's Last-Minute Wife

The Outrageous Accardi Brothers

The Christmas He Claimed the Secretary
The Accidental Accardi Heir

Visit the Author Profile page
at Harlequin.com for more titles.

To Jackie, because writing with you is always so much fun!

CHAPTER ONE

PROUD ASTERION TERAS gazed down at the elegant and diminutive old woman before him in dark, arrogant astonishment, his default expression. "I beg your pardon?"

"You heard me," his grandmother replied. Her gaze was canny and sharp, as ever. She sat in her favorite chair as if it was a throne, but Asterion was not the sort to bend a knee to anyone, not even the matriarch of what was left of his family. Then she said the same astounding thing again. "You need a wife. Badly."

"I can think of nothing I require less, Yia Yia," Asterion replied dryly.

And that should have been the end of the matter, but he knew very well it was not.

He looked across the elegant, airy room that offered views of the island from all sides with the Mediterranean gleaming in the distance. The Teras villa had been the family's prize jewel for generations, sitting on the estate that some glorious ancestor or another had won by finding favor with a long-ago king.

The villa was unofficially known as his grandmother's castle, high on the most sought-after hill with one of the finest views around of the whole of the island kingdom. And these days, Dimitra Teras was more than happy to consider herself a sort of queen of all she surveyed.

Given that Dimitra was one of the few residents of the island who could boast of a friendship with the actual queen, who was rarely seen in public any longer, no one would dare question her on this.

Not even Asterion, who otherwise questioned everyone. On everything. As if it was his duty.

He sometimes thought it was.

His twin brother, Poseidon, stood by one of the far windows, and Asterion could tell from the set to his twin's shoulders that Poseidon was no more interested in a potential wife than he was. It was a topic of some amusement for the both of them that while newspapers and ambitious strangers were forever intimating that there was strife between the two heirs to the Teras family fortune, the brothers actually enjoyed each other's company.

They were a mere minute apart, after all.

But they preferred not to let the truth get out—not when it was far more entertaining to read reports of their nonexistent enmity instead. The reality was that Asterion and Poseidon had competed for everything because they liked competing. They had each taken to their part of the family empire with the competitive spirit that had marked their relationship since the womb, according to their mother, who they could both remember telling them stories of what she was certain had been brawls while tucked away in her belly.

They'd lost her in the same car accident that had taken their father and grandfather, too, when the twins were twelve.

Asterion preferred not to think about unpleasant things he couldn't change. Particularly that. Not when he could still recall the jolt of impact. And worse, what came after.

"Both of you," Dimitra was saying, with an unfortunate sort of ring in her voice, as if she was issuing proclamations. "The pair of you are little better than wolves. From day to day, I don't know which one of you has the worst reputation."

At this, Poseidon laughed. "I have endeavored to make certain it was me."

"Nonsense," Asterion responded, lifting a brow. "What are you but everyone's favorite playboy? A mere trinket, to be used and discarded."

"Not all of us take pride in being considered the Monster of the Mediterranean, *ton megalýtero adelfó,*" Poseidon replied with his usual ease.

Poseidon smiled. Asterion brooded. They had been thus since birth.

"I am old," their grandmother announced. Which was a shocking statement from a woman who had previously made it clear that she intended to defy the ravages of age by remaining immortal. Asterion had not doubted her. Now, as both of her grandsons stared at her, she smiled. In a manner that could only be called dangerous. "Death stalks me even now."

"Only last week you made a great song and dance out of the fact your doctors told you that you are healthier than the average thirty-year-old," Asterion said. "Or have you forgotten? Is that the sort of stalking you mean?"

"I wish that I could gracefully recede into the shrouds of a foggy memory," Dimitra replied crisply. "Sadly, my mind is all too sharp. I see the two of you with perfect clarity. I am forced to read about your exploits daily, and I am not a young woman. I have no intention of seeing this family die out simply because the two of you are so useless."

"Useless," Poseidon repeated, with that laugh of his that one tabloid had once called more dangerous than an earthquake, such was its seductive power. "I'm not sure the shareholders would agree, Yia Yia."

"Last I checked," Asterion said in agreement, "Poseidon's Hydra Shipping and my own Minotaur Group far exceed the average annual earnings of any other member of this family. Ever. Not only this year, Yia Yia—every year. But you know this."

"You demand this," Poseidon murmured.

Dimitra pretended not to hear him. "I want great-grandchildren," she replied, waving a hand as if accomplishments in the corporate world mattered little to her.

When Asterion knew all too well that Dimitra Teras had a keen business mind that she never hesitated to use as a weapon, taking her competitors out at the knees.

Where did she imagine he and his brother had learned it?

"Are you well?" he asked, while Poseidon only laughed. They were identical, but no one had any trouble telling them apart. The same dark hair. The same blue eyes the color of the sea all around them. But one of them never smiled. The other never stopped. "Since when have you been domestic?"

"It has nothing to do with domesticity, *paidiá,*" their grandmother replied.

Children. As if Asterion and Poseidon were toddlers, clambering about in short pants.

No one else would dare speak to two of the most powerful men in the world in this fashion. No one else ever had. Their exploits and accomplishments were known the world over. Business rivals surrendered rather than attempt to fight them. Women flung themselves at their feet. Since their twelfth birthday, there had only ever been one person with the audacity to suggest to them that they, too, were mortal beings.

And she was laying it on a bit thick today.

"The sad truth I have come to accept is that neither one of you can be trusted to find suitable mates," Dimitra was saying now, in a particularly long-suffering way that suggested she was enjoying herself. "Far too dissolute, the pair of you, for all that you come at it differently." The brothers eyed each other, but could not argue. "Nor can either one of you be trusted to take care of things in a reasonable amount of time. I would like to see my great-grandchildren, if only to ensure that they are brought up properly. This has nothing to do with my severe concerns about your characters, and everything to do with the family legacy."

The brothers gazed at each other once more, then aimed that look at her.

"We are the family legacy," Asterion said quietly.

Dimitra sniffed. "I have given you both many hints over the years, none of which you have appeared to notice. So this time I will speak to you in a language I know you understand." She leaned forward in her chair, clasping her hands together so that her many priceless jewels caught the light and sent it spinning this way and that, as if she controlled that, too. "You will each marry the woman of my choosing, or I will make certain that your inheritance is left to an outsider rather than split between you. An outsider who will then, lest you have forgotten, have a controlling interest in the family trust."

Asterion made a disapproving sound. "We have not forgotten."

"You hate outsiders more than we do," Poseidon reminded her.

"The choice is yours," Dimitra said resolutely.

And smiled, a bit too cat-with-the-canary for Asterion. If it had been anyone but his much-beloved grandmother saying such things to him, he would simply have turned on his heel, left her presence, and set about destroying her. But he loved his grandmother—and not only because he knew too well that she did not make idle threats.

And besides, she was their only weak spot. They had made their own fortunes. They had carved their own paths. She was the only family they had left after the accident and she had cared for them ever since. In her own inimitable way, certainly, but Asterion did not have to consult with Poseidon to know they still felt as they always had.

If Dimitra wanted a legacy, they would give her one.

However grudgingly.

She waited, as if she expected explosions. Crockery tossed against walls, fists through walls—but she had not raised them to be so obvious.

Dimitra smiled wider when all they did was wait. "I want to be very clear that this is under my control, not yours. You both must agree to both woo and marry the women I select for you."

Again, the twins looked at each other, communicating without words.

"You say this as if it is some hardship for us to woo women, Yia Yia," Poseidon drawled. "I do not wish to make you blush, but this has not been a great challenge for either one of us. Ever."

"I said *woo and then marry,*" Dimitra replied tartly. "I did not say *seduce and then discard.* And these will not be those dreadful cardboard creatures the two of you favor. You need a good woman, each of you. And in the interests of full disclosure, I will share with you that I do not believe either one of you is capable of gaining the regard of a decent woman."

There was a glint her eyes, the same blue as theirs. "Given that you never have."

Asterion was frowning. "I don't understand why you would risk the family legacy over something as silly as *wooing* and *marrying*."

"The two of you are miserable, whether you know it or not," she said, and shook her head, even though her eyes yet gleamed. "Too powerful for your own good, too set in your ways, and what do you have to show for it? Brokenhearted women of low caliber trail about behind you, telling appalling tales of your treatment of them."

"No one complains of the way we treat them," Poseidon said. "Rather that we do not continue treating them that way as long as they would like us to."

Dimitra didn't *quite* roll her eyes. "You are forever in the tabloids, one scandal after the next, and trust me when I tell you that at a certain point you will be considered irredeemable by any decent woman."

Poseidon laughed. "You say that as if it is a bad thing."

"You have responsibilities to this family and its continuing legacy, Poseidon," she shot back. "And at present you are on the verge of being known as little more than a silly whore."

In another family, that might have been an insult. But Poseidon only laughed.

"Never a *silly* whore, surely."

Dimitra turned her glare on Asterion. "Meanwhile, you delight in brooding about like something out of a gothic mystery, when the only real mystery is how any female alive confuses that for anything but the worst kind of narcissism. No one is interested in your pain, Asterion. It is not a personality, it is an affectation."

Asterion lifted a brow at her, ignoring his twin's laughter. "Not all of us are charming, Yia Yia. Some of us must be challenging instead."

"I've made my decision," Dimitra shot back. "And you must decide right now, as death could take me at any moment." She was literally flushed with good health, but neither one of them argued. So she went on. "Either surrender your inheritance entirely, or, for once in your life, do as you're told."

The brothers looked at each other and for a moment, all was still.

But they communicated the way they always had. And Asterion could see his own reaction reflected in his brother's eyes.

How bad could it be? Poseidon asked silently.

Asterion remembered his parents' marriage and knew it could be very bad indeed. Terrible, even.

But he decided, then and there, that while he might acquiesce to the trappings of this farce if it would please his grandmother—and he knew he would always do what he could to please Dimitra, old dragon though she was, and within reason—he had no intention of allowing any of the other things people were always trumpeting on about when it came to marriage to ensnare him. Connection. Intimacy.

He was not built for such things and would not permit them anywhere near him. And as he thought that, he knew it to be true, for there was so far nothing in his life that he could not control. And nothing he did not control, even his grandmother.

For she might think she was getting the upper hand here, but Asterion knew full well she could not force either one of them to any altar.

The fact of the matter was that the Teras legacy needed heirs.

It was all the better that he was to be provided with a suitable bride so he could make that happen and then carry on as he always had, doing precisely as he pleased in pursuit of his goals.

Not that he would tell his grandmother this. She was a Teras, after all. She also liked to win.

As for the potential bride, he was unconcerned. Women were like dessert. Fluffy, sugary, quickly consumed, and easily forgotten.

Asterion had to assume the "decent" ones were too, perhaps beneath a few layers of tedious virtue.

He indicated this, more or less, to his brother. Silently.

He and Poseidon, in perfect accord, nodded. Then they turned back to their grandmother, who sat in her chair looking nothing but serene.

"We will marry the brides of your choice, of course," Asterion said.

Forbiddingly, but that only made Dimitra seem to glow.

"Someone should notify the press," Poseidon added. "As I expect there will be much lamenta-

tion. Wailing in the streets, rending of garments—
the usual."

But Dimitra Teras only smiled, as if she knew
something they didn't.

When surely that was impossible.

CHAPTER TWO

BRITA MARTIS ONLY returned to her father's sad, ruined house that night out of necessity.

That was the only reason she ever went back.

She had spent the better part of this last year camping out in the wildest reaches of the land that her family had stopped pretending to care for generations back. As a child she had crept about the property, looking for the ruins of the old gardens in the tangles of greenery and creeping vines, and trying to find the maze of hedges she'd seen old drawings of in some of the unused rooms.

Even then she had been avoiding her family as much as possible.

These days she preferred to spend her time with the creatures who lived in the wild thickets and dense forests all over the old hills, because she'd always considered them her real family and the woodlands her true home. Brita found fangs and claws and the odd sting significantly more pleasant than spending time with any of the people she was related to by blood, all of whom lived in the old villa—made more of regret and dashed dreams these days than the crumbling, whitewashed stones.

It was late in the evening and she crept in from the untended sprawl of gardens gone wild slowly. Carefully. Because she had learned that it was far better to know exactly where her father, stepmother, and haughty cousins were than to come upon them unexpectedly or unprepared. That never seemed to go well. It was all slings and arrows, hideous accusations and terrible scenes. She had been heartily sick of the lot of them long ago.

After three years away from her family and their demands, this last year of more contact had been a lot harder than she'd remembered it.

Tonight, she only needed to replenish her supplies and do a bit of laundry. Then she intended to head straight out again, long before dawn. Because she liked to avoid anyone she was related to at all costs and also because she was never happier than when she was sleeping beneath the sky with the wildlife she loved near.

Who needed the questionable ties of her blood relatives when she had all that?

She crossed the wild grass and melted into the shadows at the side of the old villa that had been little more than a shadow of its once resplendent self since well before Brita was born. Something she only knew from the dusty old photographs she'd found in boxes in abandoned rooms here, because it was a fact that no one in her family had taken much care of the place in as long as anyone could remember.

Taking care of the historic villas of this island kingdom took funds that her family preferred to spend on themselves. The wiring was treacherous if it existed at all, the roof leaked, and there were mice in the walls, but her stepmother drove an aspirational car and could swan about in fashionable clothes in the glitzy beach communities.

The old villa stood, cracked and diminished and largely ignored, as the perfect monument to what had become of the Martis family.

Brita had always related more to the building than her blood. If it was up to her, she would kick out all the parasitical people and give it to the animals she preferred. Sometimes she dreamed she did just that.

The doors and windows were all flung open to let the soft, breezy Mediterranean night inside. Brita knew at a glance that this was not because her father and stepmother, or any of her grasping cousins, had particular affinity for the outdoors. Or cared much for fresh air, for that matter.

It was usually because there was precious little money for air-conditioning, and the house got stifling in the evenings—and they did need to keep the skeleton staff on, lest they be forced to fend for themselves, which meant at least *some* attention to said skeleton staff's well-being. So they opened all the windows and pretended they liked it that way, and far better than noisy machines.

Brita never had to pretend. The sea was *just there*, forever in the corner of everyone's eye no matter where they cared to look, and breezes were plentiful. Especially when she was on one of the cliff tops she considered her very own living room, surrounded by the flora and fauna that were all the family she needed.

And who were also a good deal quieter of an evening.

She had learned how to move silently and unseen a long time ago, a skill she used to track wildlife all over the island kingdom these days, the better to rehabilitate the wounded, observe the habits of the healthy, and find her friends. Her own family members were easy game in comparison.

They also made *a lot* more noise.

"Something needs to be done, Vasilis," came her stepmother's voice in the hectoring tone she used all the time but specifically liked to aim at Brita's father. "There is only a month or two left before this trial year of hers is at an end. And then what will become of us? She swans off into a nunnery and we go into the poorhouse?"

As usual, they were discussing Brita.

Out in the dark, she sighed. Quietly.

Had everything gone according to plan—or at least, according to how it had always been since she was a child—they all would have ignored Brita entirely. Her mother had run off from Vasilis when Brita was small and had proven herself unequal to the task of mothering from afar. Or perhaps it was that she had taken her escape when she could, and Brita was simply collateral damage. In any case, she had removed herself from the island and never looked back. Last Brita had heard from her—in a very strange email sometime last year—she was *following her bliss* on a yoga retreat in Indonesia that had so far lasted for *four whole trips around the sun*.

Vasilis had remarried with alacrity. And her new stepmother, the perpetually victimized Nikoletta, had at first wanted to see as little of Brita as possible.

A state of affairs which had suited young Brita just fine.

Brita still thought of those years as glorious, really. She had still been a child and had been left to run about the estate as she pleased. The Martis family, once a part of the aristocracy on this little island kingdom plunked down in the Mediterranean not far from the Greek mainland, had long since lost any of the wealth that had once gone along with their station. So while her father and stepmother and cousins all plotted out various ways to regain it that did not involve lowering themselves to *work* of any kind, Brita had been left to her own devices.

She had greatly enjoyed her own devices.

But then, sadly, it had become more and more clear that she was going to be quite pretty. There had been endless discussions about it. Every time she came in from a carefree tramp about in the woodlands and over the hills she would find them all *peering* at her, but since she considered the lot of them odd—and odder by the day the more she got to know the far friendlier and more approachable wildlife—she'd assumed they'd get bored and stop.

Instead, it got worse. Because as time went on and

adolescence enhanced her looks instead of stealing them away into the more typical awkwardness, Brita turned out to be actually rather beautiful.

It had been a disaster.

Overnight, she had been forbidden from roaming the grounds—much less farther afield. She had gone from raising herself as she liked to having an unpleasant committee overseeing her every breath.

Because every last one of her relatives suddenly needed to rail on about every last detail about Brita and her appearance, from her clothing to her manners to her style of speech. She had been unable to walk three steps without stinging critiques on all sides. It had been as baffling as it was a complete shift from all she knew, and no one had explained it to her.

But soon enough, the reason for this shift became clear.

She'd overheard it in much the same manner as tonight. Because her family liked to sit about tossing back the *ouzo* while Brita preferred to keep her wits about her—and, if possible, from a protected vantage point. Like every other child in all of history, she'd been scolded that eavesdroppers never heard a good word about themselves, but then, she wasn't looking for praise.

Brita was always and ever looking for information, since she was never given explanations. And sooner or later, her garrulous and indiscreet relatives always shouted out the things she wanted to hear when they thought she was tucked away in bed.

It was like a fairy tale, she discovered. The bad parts of the real fairy tales.

Because her family had decided that since Brita was so shockingly and unexpectedly beautiful, all they needed to do to solve their ever-growing financial problems was to marry her off to a suitably rich man. And the more beautiful she got with each passing year, the more wild their fantasies became as they imagined the ways this future wealthy husband of hers would be beholden to the family, a victim to her beauty forevermore.

They were certain they could raise their fortunes from the grave that easily.

The first attempt to hurry up and get her married off had come when she turned eighteen.

On her birthday, her older cousins had produced a selection of suitors, all of them of a certain social class and each less appealing than the last.

Brita had appealed to her stepmother's ambition, taking care to act as if *she* didn't care either way. That was the key, she had learned long ago. The very hint of any emotion and Nikoletta would instantly do the opposite of whatever it was Brita asked, forever on the lookout for ways she could punish her stepdaughter for being the walking, talking reminder of the wife Vasilis liked only in retrospect. And only when drunk.

That time she'd kept her composure and her gambit had worked. She'd been permitted to get an education because, as she'd argued, she needed to learn how to conduct herself in the company of the sorts of great men she knew her stepmother fancied *should* wish to align themselves with the Martis family's spotless pedigree.

The family had skipped her university graduation and, in lieu of the traditional celebration, had presented her instead with the suitor they had chosen for her to wed. This time, they had colluded. Instead of presenting her with a selection, they had all decided that the man in question was the only one who would do.

He was significantly older. Her father's age, if not ten years on. And while he had not been unkind—already an upgrade from the original set of suitors—he had reminded Brita of the sort of unfortunate fish that could only be found deep beneath the sea, wall-eyed and pasty.

All of which would have made her think twice had she wanted to marry him, but Brita had never had any intention of marrying this man. Or any man. And though she had spent her university years keeping her own counsel, so as not to engage in the unnecessary squabbles her family viewed as sport, she hadn't been able to keep her revulsion in.

One day, while her cousins were sitting around arguing over which famous personages they would invite to the wedding reception, despite not knowing any of them personally, and her father and stepmother were toasting their success, Brita had looked up from her own dinner—made separately in the kitchens by the staff, who she also considered more her family than this lot, because she could not eat the meat of the creatures she cared for—and smiled.

Politely, she had thought.

I will not marry him, she said. Very simply.

Don't be childish, Nikoletta had snapped back at once, slamming her glass down on the scarred surface of the old table, the scene of many an operatic family battle. *You'll do what you're told.*

Brita had made sure to take a moment and look each of them in the eye, one after the next, to make certain they were all paying attention. *I won't.*

They had not taken this pronouncement well.

There had been the usual shouting and screaming, and much damage to objects and walls. There had been threats aplenty. They had locked her in her room, because they knew so little about her that they were unaware that she had been sneaking out into the hills since she was small. They had told her that she would no longer be allowed the *privilege* of the vegetarian food she preferred, and she'd heard them chortling about that cruelty while in their cups, because they had no idea that it wasn't only Brita who viewed the long-suffering staff with great fondness. The staff liked her back. They would never keep food from her. They simply made sure she got it in secret, usually when she crept into the kitchens to eat with them, as she had been doing since she was small. Far better than attempting to digest anything in the midst of the usual nightly battles.

This nonsense went on for a whole summer.

In the end, Vasilis had given her an ultimatum.

You will marry this man or you will become a nun, destined to live out your days in a convent, with nothing to do but pray for deliverance. Do you understand me?

Brita had packed her bags for the local convent that night.

And rather than being the punishment her father imagined, Brita found her time as a novitiate quite pleasant. She liked the schedule of the days and the solitude of so much prayer. She liked the company and her shared labor with the sisters in the convent gardens and kitchens. There were never any temper tantrums. There were no tedious scenes.

No one was ever drunk and disorderly.

But the best part of the convent was that the sisters were far more interested in who Brita was as a person and what gifts she could bring to bear in her time with them than her family ever had been.

Not one of them seemed to notice or care that she was beautiful.

Instead, they asked her about her dreams. And when she told them that she had always wanted nothing more than to open some sort of wildlife sanctuary here on the island, they hadn't laughed in her face like her cousins, or angrily dismissed her like her father and stepmother.

On the contrary. The sisters loved the idea.

Instead of being a punishment, being consigned to a life of monasticism was the freest Brita had felt around other people since she had been a largely ignored child.

But the order did not allow anyone to take more permanent vows without first making absolutely certain that giving her life to the church in this way was right for her.

I know it's right, Brita had argued, because she would have been happy never to see her relatives again.

But the Abbess had only smiled in her serene way. *You must take this year not to ask what it is* you *know, child. But instead what it is that He requires of you.*

It was that part of her life of piety that Brita found the most challenging. The looking for answers instead of making her own as she went along.

Still, she had gamely gone off to test herself in the world.

That was the point of the trial year, the sisters had all assured her. To go and tempt herself with everything that the world had to offer, all the things she enjoyed that had no part in convent life, so she could decide if this quiet life of contemplation was truly for her.

Brita had spent the year wandering through the wildest parts of the island, taking note of all the animals and birds and assorted creatures who lived there, making friends with some of them and helping those who needed it. It had been a long year, but a good one, and she was looking forward to the life she planned to build in the convent.

She had almost forgotten that her family was opposed to that life. They had expected her to beg them to let her come home, but she never had. Maybe it wasn't really a shock to discover that they were still bound and determined to marry her off anyway, whether she liked it or not.

But out here in the shadows, where she had always been—where she preferred to be—it felt like a rather large shock all the same.

Since she couldn't recall the last time any one of them had bothered to have so much as a conversation with her, how could they be so certain that she would obey them? Why would she want to when they had never been able to even feign a passing interest in her—aside from what her assortment of features could buy them?

"Exactly how much of her input is really required?" one of her older cousins asked in his oily way. "Surely we can slip her a few pills and be done with it. She wouldn't be the first bride in the world who was less than *compos mentis* at her own nuptials."

"This is the modern age," another agreed. "Surely the priest can be bribed like anyone else."

It was probably only that she hadn't heard them talk about her in a while now—a deliberate choice on her part that she underscored by staying far away—that their words landed so hard. Brita sighed a little, shook it off, and then made her way around to the far side of the old house. None of the family ever bothered with this wing of the villa. It had been closed off in her grandfather's day, with sheets thrown over all the furniture that hadn't been sold and bartered away to pay the bills over the years.

This was the part of the villa she liked. This part had always been hers. Where her cousins saw sad old ghosts of lost splendor, Brita saw her happiest memories. Playing tag with the cook. Hiding out with old photographs. Reading her way through every book about the island and its wildlife she could find.

At some point, Vasilis would have to start selling off parts of the Martis estate, and that would break her heart, because to him it was nothing but land, but to her it was worlds within worlds, a universe of memories and comfort, furry friends and feathered things who watched over her when no one else ever had.

Eventually he would have to sell the villa, too, and she was all too aware that no potential buyer was likely to take on such an overwhelming renovation project. They were far more likely to knock the place down and put in condos in this neglected part of the island where tourists never ventured.

Brita didn't like to think about it.

Instead, she called on one of the most important lessons she'd learned from her many, many hours in this abandoned part of the house. That being her encyclopedic knowledge of which windows were never latched. And which were accessible even if they were.

She pulled one open now, hoisted herself onto the ledge, then swung herself inside.

Another skill her childhood had taught her was

how to move like a ghost through the house itself, and the staff liked her too much to react to the way she slipped in and out of rooms as she wished, sometimes spooking them when she did. She did a load of laundry, avoided her stepmother tottering down the hallway muttering about *faded glory,* and took a long bath. Then she dressed again, packed up the supplies she needed in her bag, and made her way down to the kitchen with her beloved quiver and bow over her shoulder.

"They've all gone a bit mad tonight," the cook, Maria, murmured when Brita came in. "You know what they're like. Too much *tsipouro* and they think it's a feudal system around here."

"The last time I came home, I suggested that Cousin Panagiota do the marrying," Brita reminded her. Both she and Maria laughed at that notion. "Since she is so big on the idea."

"As if madam would ever submit herself to such an indignity." Maria hooted. "Besides, she still thinks she's going to trade on the Martis name and snag herself one of the few remaining nobles cluttering up the hills."

Brita rolled her eyes and settled in for one of her favorite sorts of discussions—in this case, a philosophical exploration of what nobility even meant on an island like this, where everyone knew that the real power was in the wealth and consequence of men like the mighty Teras brothers, who were known the world over and regularly appeared in flashy events with famous people, or so everyone told her every time their names were mentioned.

She personally wouldn't know a Teras brother if she tripped over one of them.

These days, the island was still a kingdom—but in name only. She couldn't remember the last time the old queen had even bothered to cast an eye outside her fancy palace. Why should she? The island ran on tourism, commerce, and the influx of wealthy businessmen who wanted nothing more than to get in with corporate giants like the Minotaur Group and Hydra Shipping, both Teras family enterprises.

In her more charitable moments, which came along more rarely these days, she thought it was a sad sort of disappointment that her family was so determined to cling to a way of life that had never been theirs in the first place. Not in any of their lifetimes, anyway.

But before she and Maria could really get into what was one of their favorite topics for long nights in this very kitchen, a man appeared.

One moment it was just her and Maria and the villa's old kitchen, where they had spent many an evening together when Brita was supposedly confined to her bedchamber, confident that none of the rest of the family would ever demean themselves by entering a place where grubby scrub work was done by servants.

Brita had hoisted herself up on one of the counters, and was swinging her feet against the cabinets below her, snacking on a bit of bread and cheese that Maria had slid her way.

But suddenly and without warning the man appeared, and she froze.

And the only thing that had ever felt the way she did in this moment was when she'd been caught out in a storm last summer. She'd miscalculated and had found herself with no cover, but she hadn't panicked.

Instead, she'd been forced to surrender herself to the rain, the wind, the crack of lightning high over the island's hills.

And it hadn't felt like a surrender at all.

She'd felt elemental. Alive.

As if she was a part of the same great upheaval as the storm that crashed through the sky. As if it lived in her.

Some part of her thought it had, ever since, and now she looked at this man in the kitchen doorway and could see that same *immensity*.

That same intense, awe-inducing electricity.

She felt shocked straight through, the way she had when lightning had forked across the sky *just there*—so close she could nearly *touch* it—making her skin burn, but tonight that burning was inside as well as out.

It was all a kind of narrowing spiral, tighter and tighter, and it landed like heat between her legs.

"Begging your pardon, sir," Maria said in a far more polite tone of voice that anything Brita could imagine attempting to get out, even if the old queen herself had appeared before her in all her finery. "But

I think you might have lost your way. The family are all gathered in the other part of the house."

But Brita hardly heard her. She couldn't seem to look away from the man before her, who hadn't moved from the threshold, yet still seemed to crowd the rambling kitchen.

Until everything was airless.

Particularly her.

He was so *severe,* she thought. No one to be trifled with.

All he did was stand there, and though the way he held his body should have seemed nonchalant, it wasn't.

Nothing about him is casual, she found herself thinking, the way she would about any wild thing, and no matter that this one wore a dark suit that whispered of wealth and consequence instead of a pelt or some fur.

There was an intensity that rippled within him, and from him.

He gazed at Maria for a long moment, acknowledging her, and then he shifted that gaze to Brita. And held it there.

Lightning struck again, hard and deep.

"I'm not here for the family," he said, and the way he looked at her, Brita thought he knew. She thought he knew every crackle of that lightning that struck her again and again, every kiss of electricity and wonder. "I'm here for you."

CHAPTER THREE

IT WAS WORSE—much worse—than Asterion had anticipated.

And his expectations had been markedly low.

When Dimitra explained to him who she expected him to marry, he stared at her as if she had taken leave of her senses at last. He almost said as much. He almost suggested that time came inexorably for everyone, and perhaps her razor-sharp intellect was not the weapon it had once been.

He restrained himself. By a hair.

"I do not understand the resistance," his grandmother replied, though her dark eyes danced. "Brita Martis is a young woman of great virtue. You would be lucky indeed if she were to lower herself to the likes of you."

"She is a nun," Asterion said shortly. "An actual nun, Yia Yia."

"Best of luck to you then," she replied smoothly. "You like to consider yourself a god among men, do you not? Now is your chance to prove that you are equal to the god she has already pledged to follow."

There had been nothing for it but to seek out the

paragon in question. And the fact that the woman was an untouched saint was not what bothered the decidedly sinful Asterion the most when he set out to deliver the good news to her—that he would be changing her life for the better.

It was that the woman in question wasn't even in residence in said nunnery to receive him or her own great luck. When he had gone there, doing his best to appear the part of the besotted suitor—or really, any man who wasn't him and might therefore do things like seek out women instead of brush them off in droves—the nun who stood in the doorway and denied him entrance told him that Brita was not there.

He had not allowed for that possibility. He had, at first, been unable to take it on board. Surely nuns remained in their nunneries instead of roaming about. That was, as far as Asterion was aware, the purpose of herding them into monastic collectives in the first place.

"Brita is out on her trial year, as it happens," the nun before him told him with an unhurriedness that made it clear she answered to no earthly man, and certainly not to the likes of Asterion. "Her last hurrah, if you will." When Asterion stared back at her blankly, she continued in the same untroubled manner. "It is a whole year in which to immerse herself in all of the world's temptations to see if she can find her way back to the Lord."

He had always imagined that these places preferred to lock the world out forever and hide away from it, fearful that any stray hint of its existence outside their prayers would bring all their devils crashing in with vengeance aplenty. It was fascinating that these nuns went in the opposite direction, but he did not wish to find himself fascinated by a nun. Or any other creature so wholly unimpressed with him. "And if she does not?"

The austere sister eyed him in a manner that reminded him entirely too much of Dimitra. "Then she has a different path to walk than ours, with our blessing. We will pray for her."

Asterion decided this plot twist was a good thing. If she was off kicking up her heels in the sorts of clubs and bars that crowded the beaches here, the places where all the ill-behaved tourists liked to congregate while addled on drink and too much sunshine, all the better. It was always possible his grandmother had been mistaken about this woman's virtue.

Despite what she herself professed to believe and claimed could be easily proven, his grandmother was not, in fact, infallible.

After some investigating, Asterion had not liked finding out that as far as anyone could tell, Brita Martis was some sort of virgin huntress. She was rumored to be as uncivilized as the animals she cared for, roaming the hills of the island like a wild thing with a bow and her arrows. Like something out of a myth.

Not that she hunted animals. It was strongly suggested that said bow and its arrows were entirely for making certain that men did not bother her.

And they did not.

Those were the sorts of stories that were told about her in the villages. That sometimes, on a full moon, you could see Brita roaming the hills, flanked by wolves and deer and all manner of woodland creatures.

Some said they were her friends. Some claimed they were her army.

What everyone agreed on was that no matter how wild Brita might be, she was still better than her family, who lived on top of each other in that falling-down old villa out on the far side of the island, dreaming of glory days past.

Dimitra had always had a wicked sense of humor.

Asterion had never been much for hunting in the wilderness when there were empires to topple instead, though he had to believe the principles were the same. Tonight, he had waited about outside the Martis villa as he had done for nearly a week now. All of the information he and his people had collected had indicated that she returned to the family estate now and again, but none of his sources thought it particularly credible she would march in the front door and interact with her family in the normal way when she otherwise went to such lengths to avoid them.

He'd been beginning to think she was nothing more than a figment of everyone's overwrought imaginations when he'd seen her at last, slipping across the grounds from the untended mess of former gardens that tangled their way off into the hills.

She kept to the shadows outside the villa's windows, pausing briefly before going on around toward the back. He'd followed at a distance, circling until he saw her inside. Nowhere near the reception rooms at the front, where the liquor flowed freely, but in the back with the servants.

He was not one to lurk about now that his quarry was in sight, and so he walked straight in.

Then stopped, as if held in place by an unseen hand.

He might have found that an outrage to be addressed, but he could not focus on it. Because she stared at him, and he stared back.

And that seemed to take a very long while.

Asterion could not wait to ask his grandmother what on earth she'd been thinking.

For Brita Martis was exactly as wild as it had been said she was. Maybe more.

Her black hair flowed all about her, part of it still wet, a mess of unruly waves that fell nearly to her waist. He had expected to find her wearing the hides of animals, dirt and twigs, and so it was a slight disappointment that she was dressed reasonably enough in what looked like tactical hiking trousers, a form-fitting tank top, and a button-down shirt that was falling off one of her slender shoulders.

She had obviously just bathed, so perhaps the dirt, twigs, and skins were next on the sartorial agenda, but that wasn't the trouble here.

It wasn't even that she wore her *otherness* like the skins she'd left off tonight, visible in the way she sat, the way she stared back at him, the way she *breathed*.

The real trouble with Brita Martis, which no one had bothered to mention to him, was that she was objectively beautiful.

Just...beautiful. Astonishingly so.

Stunning, to be more precise.

Asterion, who had long prided himself on his cynicism and his immunity to the usual blandishments of attractive women, recognized that he was actually *stunned.*

Nothing could have appalled him more.

Her face was like a work of art, the kind involving oil and paint and old masters, or perhaps the sensual touch of marble. Her hair was black, her eyes were a kind of brilliant bronze and gold, and everything else about her a pageant of symmetry and feminine glory. With sensual lips that made him hunger to taste her, and the hint of supple curves. He had the sudden thought that it was no wonder she would rather spend time with wild animals, because surely every man who gazed upon her became little more than a slavering beast at the sight.

He was close to such a display himself, when Asterion had always been about control. It wasn't a *preference*, it was a *necessity*, because he had seen where letting go led. He had been in the same car that had killed most of his family, and he remembered the fiery, passionate, high-decibel relationship his parents had indulged in that had caused it.

He had vowed that he would never allow himself such a loss of restraint.

He had never imagined that vow would be tested.

In all his days and the many women he'd sampled, it never had been.

Which was to say, he had never stared at a woman before as if he'd been cut in two.

As if there was a great divide between all that had come before, and now.

Having seen her.

As if that simple act had changed him, Asterion Teras, who was like the great rock where he'd built his house and started his business—always the same impossibly hard surface, impervious to the attempts of time and weather to alter him in any way.

He felt something roar in him, deep.

As if he was no rock after all but another wild thing, and here she was, the local myth all wild things followed—

But Asterion followed no one. He was only doing his grandmother's bidding at present because it had to do with his fortune. His legacy.

The only things he cared about.

His fortune because he controlled it ruthlessly and made it do what he liked.

His legacy because it mattered to Dimitra, and she was the only woman who mattered to him, or ever would.

He told himself it had nothing at all to do with the heat and ache in his sex and the urge he had to roar out these strange things inside him like the beast he'd never been. To tear down this villa if he had to and carry her off—

But he was not one of the storybook creatures

the villagers claimed followed her about adoringly or became her minions every full moon, depending.

Though he thought he would never know how it was he didn't give in to the urge to become one, there in the door to that rumpled, ancient kitchen.

"I need your help," he told her instead, sounding quite pleasant and conversational to his ear. And though he had planned to say that all along, it was a little more close to the truth than he liked. "You are Brita Martis, are you not? The nun who can charm any animal she sees?"

He could see she liked that description. She tilted her head slightly, though her gaze was solemn. "I'm not a nun. Nor an animal charmer. Though I am Brita Martis, all the same. That part is true enough."

"There's something crying on the cliffs near my home," he told her, giving the words the same sort of solemnity. "It's been going on some while. I was told that you might be the one who can find the source of the sound and perhaps save the poor creature, whatever it is."

There were no cries. He was lying—though he preferred to think it not quite a *lie*. It was, instead, a deliberate snare. A little trap, that was all.

"And you tracked me down here?" She lifted her chin. "Most people do not present themselves around the back of a stranger's house in the middle of the night. Or perhaps things are different wherever it is you live, Mr....?"

It had been a long while since someone failed to recognize him on sight. Asterion wasn't sure he believed that it was a possibility, not on this island where his family was more recognizable than the queen, since they actually ventured out into daylight from time to time.

And, of course, everyone knew what had happened to them. And more, what he and Poseidon had made out of that wreckage.

Whether it was a slight or sheer ignorance, he ignored it. "I would have gone to the front door, but there were no lights on. When I followed the sounds I heard around the side, there appeared to be a great many people arguing in one of the rooms." He made an ineffective sort of gesture that felt entirely wrong, which was how he knew that he should lean into it. That had been his grandmother's only advice, such as it was.

Try to be something other than who you are, she had told him. *You catch more flies with honey than with vinegar, child.*

Though he did not think she could possibly know if that was so, having embodied all that was vinegar for the whole of her life. "So I kept going until I found you here."

Some women would blush and stammer. This one did neither. "Who told you about me?"

Asterion was assaulted by the strangest sensation. On the one hand, he was obviously amazed and astonished that she didn't leap to do his bidding like everyone else did without question. On the other, it was reasonable to be suspicious of a stranger turning up as he had.

He decided he was glad that this otherworldly creature, who he must wed no matter what, was not as foolhardy as her actions had suggested she would be, gallivanting about in the hills day and night. By herself, no less.

And so he chose to answer her question. He named several shopkeepers in the biggest village on the island. After a moment, she nodded, and so he inclined his head. "I am sorry we have not had occasion to meet before. I am Asterion Teras."

Then he watched, intrigued, as her face...changed. "Oh," she murmured, exchanging a look with the red-cheeked, yet otherwise poker-faced woman at her side. "You would be. I should have known."

He would have followed that up, that artless *you would be,* but she was sliding off the counter then. And she was landing on the cracked floor with a kind of athletic litheness that made his whole body go tight. Hot.

Asterion was a big man, but she was taller than most of the local women, and he liked it. Better yet, she did not stoop her shoulders as many tall women did when they were not models or the like, trying to make themselves smaller. Her hair was curling as they spoke, making her look even wilder as it tumbled down her back. He had no trouble at all believing that she did nothing with her time but roam up and down the hills of the island, communing with nature at will.

"Come," she said to him and frowned slightly, a

good reminder that he could not stand there and stare at her like this. That it would lead nowhere good.

Or at least, not to the sort of *wooing* he knew his grandmother had in mind.

"Let's not delay if something's hurt," she said, clearly not impressed with the fact he wasn't already making tracks.

She exchanged another glance with the cook and then came toward him, making his chest feel tight—but he had taken a step or two farther inside as they'd talked. And so she only moved past him, smelling faintly of rosemary and deep green things he knew he could not name, heading out the door of the kitchen into the darkness.

Leaving him no choice but to follow her.

He chose not to acknowledge that he wanted to follow her. A lot more than he cared to admit.

And having very little to do with Dimitra's demands.

Outside, Brita took to the shadows again and he followed suit. He watched the supple way she covered ground, not seeming to react to the sound of her family's voices. They were harsh and clearly inebriated, pouring out into the night. Polluting it.

But if it bothered her, she did not seem to give a sign except for the wide berth she gave the windows.

When they were at the still dark and forbidding front of the house once more, she adjusted the bow she carried, altered the way the strap of her bag lay over her shoulder, and then made as if to head off into the hills.

"I did drive here," Asterion pointed out. "It seemed a more efficient mode of travel than a great hike through the underbrush. At this hour."

Brita looked at him. But said nothing.

"When, as you say," he continued with great piety, "there could be something hurt awaiting you."

He was not normally given to outright lies. Then again, there *could* be something hurt there. Or anywhere.

She glided beside him as he walked down the drive, then glowered at him in earnest when he stopped beside his low-slung sports car and opened the passenger door for her.

"How did that do on the drive out here?" she asked with a suspicious lack of inflection. "Last I checked, the ruts in the dirt road could swallow a bull or two whole."

"I am an excellent driver," he assured her, though he had already called his staff to make certain the car's undercarriage was checked thoroughly upon his return.

Brita did not respond, though the *way* she failed to say anything felt like a rebuke all its own. Then she slid inside the car so many simply toppled into instead, another hint of that easy physical grace that he could see might very well become intoxicating.

It was impossible not to think about…all the potential applications.

As long as he did so in an appropriately analytical fashion.

He closed the door and was glad of the walk

around to his side. He ordered himself back under control.

Not something he had ever need to concern himself with before now.

If it weren't for his grandmother's threats, he would end this right now.

He was sure he would—if he could.

The moon up above them played hide-and-seek with the clouds as he drove them across the island, down the deeply rutted dirt track that eventually led to the more accessible road hugging the coast, always kept in top shape for tourists and their holiday photographs. Then, before hitting the stretch of the most popular beaches, bristling all year round and bright tonight as they drove on the high road above them, he headed up into the hills.

Then, at last, he navigated the car—definitely not sounding its best—out onto the bluff where he'd built the house that he liked to call his labyrinth.

It hugged the cliff in a vertical drop, half in and half out of the rock face, and his own drive wound its way through a bit of wilderness. Beside him, Brita seemed content to remain silent, but she rolled down the window as they drove closer to the cliffs.

It took him a moment to realize that she was listening. Intently.

For the cries he had told her she would hear.

Asterion did not feel guilty about that. He wouldn't know the feeling anyway, he assured himself, so alien was it to him—though he rubbed absently at his chest.

He drove up to the very small part of his house that was actually on the bluff and parked, but this time, she did not wait for him to circle the vehicle to let her out. She climbed out herself and then stood there, her head cocked slightly as she listened to the wind rushing up from the sea far below. Rushing through the trees all around them. Making its own song of wildness and far-off lands as it danced where it liked.

He led her, not down into his house proper, but only on to the great garden terrace at the top that looked almost as wild as the hill behind them. It was extensively landscaped to appear so, except for the glass dome in the center that was, he could admit it, a bit much for a front door.

But Brita did not comment on it.

Unlike every other person who he had ever brought here, she did not spare even a glance for the house.

It was his very own personal feat of engineering, one twisting level after the next, crawling down into the rock and all along the outside of the cliff's sheer drop. It had been written up in too many architectural magazines to count. It was so famous that it was a stop, out in the water, for tourists on their round-the-island boat trips.

He found it…bracing that this woman he'd found in a villa that was already more or less a ruin seemed not to care. Or really even notice.

She followed after him, yet was not paying attention *to* him, and they had walked almost to the other side of the flat garden terrace—beyond which was only the cliff's edge and the sea below—before Asterion was forced to accept that he could not recall, in the whole of his existence, another situation where his mere presence was not enough to send the woman in his company into paroxysms of giddy delight.

In point of fact, Brita hardly seemed to notice that she was in his company at all. She walked beside him, but she was still listening, clearly. For the sound of a creature in distress.

He still did not consider it a *lie*. He was a powerful man used to doing what he must to achieve the results he desired. It was no more and no less than that.

There was no earthly reason why he should keep worrying the fact of it over and over in his head, like he really was this person he was playing. *He* did not waffle about. *He* made decisions, executed the appropriate actions, and dealt with the consequences as they came.

It was all part and parcel of the control he had exerted over himself and everything in his orbit since he was all of twelve.

It was this bizarre woman who was tangling things up inside him, that was all. No one had thought to give her a script. No one had ever explained to her how she ought to act in the presence of a man like him.

Clearly.

"You must know that in the villages people speak of you in tones of awe," he told her when they stopped walking, so she could stand still, continuing to both *listen* and act as if she was alone. "Some think you're a reincarnation of one of the old goddesses. An immortal huntress, worthy of sacrifice. Daily worship. The usual rituals."

He expected her to laugh a bit. Something sparkling, effortless. The way women always did when he spoke, no matter what he said. Though he thought that this, perhaps, was the first time he had ever attempted to offer a statement that was even remotely like a compliment.

Brita did not giggle. She didn't even look at him, then away, eyes glinting, the way some did.

She didn't look at him at all.

"That's very silly," she said instead. "I don't think the sisters at the convent would find that the least bit entertaining."

Then she walked on again, moving ahead of him until she stood at the very edge of his cliff, where there were only smooth, rounded stones, large enough to serve as tables or the odd sacrificial altar, in place of any kind of fence. Brita did not cringe away from the edge, nor did she make the usual comments about the house's steep drop and how dangerous this all was, this open cliff top he called home.

Instead, Brita Martis, virgin huntress and possible myth, jumped up neatly to stand on one of the rocks set there.

Only then did she look all around, taking in the sweep of rocky cliff on either side, and the lights in his labyrinth of a house, twisting its way down the steep drop.

"I can't hear anything," she said after a moment. "Are you certain this is where you were when you heard the cry?"

"I'm certain."

He had thought this the perfect way to begin this farce, but now he was doubting himself, and Asterion had no experience whatsoever with such a state. He was a Teras. He did not doubt himself. He was genetically predisposed to have not a shred of doubt, ever.

But it had not occurred to him that he could bring a woman into his presence and have her...concentrate instead on the task at hand.

It might have been lowering indeed, had he been able to process it.

"There are cats as well as birds that can make a variety of noises that sound a lot like cries of pain or terror, but neither is necessarily the case." She turned back around and gazed down at him, and he was struck, again, by her beauty. As if she truly had loosed an arrow and shot it straight into the center of his chest.

Brita looked like a kind of statue in the moonlight, carved from warm, supple marble and made into a woman by loving hands. Breezes from the hill and the sea caught at her dark tendrils and she didn't seem to mind—or notice—letting them flow about her as her eyes scanned the darkness all around them.

"I'm familiar with the sounds of seabirds," he found himself saying.

"I would think so, with the house perched up here

like its own sort of mast. I'm surprised it's not covered in—"

"As the house is an architectural marvel," Asterion found himself saying, as if he was made of a far harder stone than marble, or as if he was the sort of person who allowed himself such base, low, reactive *feelings* in the first place, "we have always felt best to keep it as free of bird droppings as possible." That gaze of hers on his, that combination of gold and silver, felt like another blow and he found himself continuing. "In consultation with all relevant authorities, of course, so as not to disturb the local bird colonies. What do you take me for?"

It was only then, standing so that she towered over him and looked down at him with her arms bare to the night—the wind in her hair, and not the faintest hint of the usual reaction he got from women anywhere visible on her face—Brita, not quite a nun, actually seemed to give him her full attention.

"I know of you," she replied. "I grew up on this island. It would be impossible to avoid tales of you and the rest of your family."

"Unlike tales of your goddess-like immortality, the stories about my family are likely true."

"I have never met a man carved from sadness and stone," she said, in that same matter-of-fact way. There was no coy glance. There was no sideways sort of smile to soften what she was saying. "That's what they say you are. But you don't look so very different from any other man. I hope you don't mind, but it's a bit of a letdown."

Asterion could scarcely credit what he was hearing. "A *letdown*?"

She nodded, but she was already turning away. Her hands were on her hips now, the better to survey the area again. "Think about it from my perspective. I spent my whole life hearing about the Monster of the Mediterranean and then here you are. Perfectly pleasant. Like everyone on this island overdosed on their own overactive imaginations."

"*Perfectly pleasant,*" Asterion echoed with all the arrogance and affront he had in him, but it had no effect. Because once again, she wasn't paying him the slightest attention. "I have been called many things in my time, Brita, but never *pleasant.*"

"I suppose it's the money," she said in that forthright way, almost as if she couldn't hear the inflection in his voice. As if she was entirely earnest, and deaf to any possible implications. "You have so very much of it that it must inspire people to make up things about you. That you're a monster. That you storm about the planet, ripping fortunes from the hands of anyone silly enough to stand against you, blah blah blah. That's easier to stomach than the truth."

"And what," he asked, because he could not seem to keep himself from it, "is the truth?"

She turned back to him then and tipped her head to one side, the way he already knew she did when she was studying a situation. Surveying it.

He did not know how to process the fact that this half-wild woman was looking at him as if he was the one in need of *explanation*. As if he was the one who made no sense.

"You were born with quite a lot of it, weren't you?" She lifted a shoulder. "Once, a very long time ago, my family also had a lot of money. But they've been spending it ever since, and now there is none. Therefore, it's all that my family talks about. If I had to guess, I'd say that no one in your family talks about money. Why bother? It's assumed to be too abundant to mention, like the sea."

This was accurate, and so Asterion couldn't say why it sat on him so heavily. He should have rejoiced that this woman who would be marrying him, and soon, despite all this nonsense, was able to read him. That she seemed to do so with a careless ease that a great many of his rivals in tense negotiations would likely kill for.

You should rejoice, he ordered himself.

But he did not. He could not, somehow.

"I know of your family," he said in turn, and less... pleasantly. "There have been members of the Martis clan on this island for a great many generations."

"And the last of them are currently hunkered down in that old villa," she agreed briskly. "Waiting for their former glory to be restored. They don't have a concrete plan, in case you wondered. The prevailing hope is that they will wake up one morning and find themselves fabulously wealthy again. And who knows? Stranger things have happened."

"Strange things happen all the while," he agreed,

unable, somehow to wrench his gaze from hers. "But generally not where vast fortunes are concerned."

She inclined her head at that, as if in agreement. Then she leaped off the rock and back onto the terrace, making scarcely any sound at all when she landed.

Asterion realized that he was impressed with her.

It was another thing he wasn't sure he'd ever felt before. It moved in him…loudly.

Like an imperative.

"Do you have a mobile?" she asked, and he was beginning to feel weary at how easily she could surprise him. But she wasn't like any other woman he'd ever encountered. For one thing, despite himself, he was the one impressed when it was normally the opposite. And she was bold, unusual, and looking at him now.

Expectantly.

"Yes," he managed to say, horrified that he was not controlling this situation the way he should. The way he controlled every other thing around him without effort. "I have a mobile. Of course I have a mobile." He had several. "Does anyone *not* have one in this day and age?"

She held out her hand instead of answering that, and he had the experience of feeling churlish, like some kind of child in a sulk, while also feeling compelled to obey her. It was another astonishment to add to the lot.

It was not a positive.

He dug in his pocket, pulled out his mobile phone, and handed it to her.

Obediently.

And then stood there, the fearsome CEO of the Minotaur Group, who had never given an inch when he could instead take the entire territory, as she helped herself to a swipe here and a type there, until she handed it straight back to him.

"Spyware?" he asked, perhaps more acerbically than warranted.

Though he would have to instruct his staff to check the mobile as well as his poor car.

"Call me when you hear the crying again," she said, with only the faintest quizzical look about the eyes to indicate she heard his comment on *spyware*.

He noted that she looked very much as if she hoped he wouldn't call her. This wild huntress who wanted nothing to do with him.

With *him*.

That thought shot through him like another one of her arrows.

"I will," he said, fighting to get back to pleasant-sounding words and vague, indecisive gestures, like the man he'd tried to pretend he was. "I appreciate you coming tonight. But if you'll forgive me, how dire are your family's circumstances? Is it the lack of funds that has you roaming the hills as you do? The rumors I heard in the villages are that you often sleep beneath the stars."

"I could stay in the villa," she said, conversationally enough, as if the state of her family was of little matter to her. Or perhaps, he thought then, it was that its dysfunction was to her what wealth was to him. Unworthy of comment, so obvious was it. He felt an unusual sensation in the region of his ribs, but ignored it, thus proving he could control *something*.

"But you see, I only had a year."

"A year?"

Until tonight, he had taken great pride in the fact that he never asked a question in a negotiation unless he already knew the answer.

She looked at him again, all of that dark gold threaded through with bronze, and he felt it like a touch. "I suppose it's a gap year of sorts. I spent three years in the convent, learning how to be a nun. This is the year we take off from all that. We are sent off to rejoin the world, to see if we really, truly want to leave it behind."

"You are not actually a nun," he said.

But he could hardly take stock of the ruckus that caused in him, because Brita smiled.

It was...not better.

It was also glorious.

The smile changed her face as if her very own moon shined down upon her, and he had already imagined too well the things he could do with her. That lithe body. That gorgeous face. The curves he could see there, adding interest to her athletic form.

But now he could imagine nothing else.

He was not sure he ever would, and he certainly didn't know what to do with that. It was nearly poetic. It was not him at all.

It was a nightmare.

Yet he could not wake.

"Almost," Brita told him. "I am *almost* a nun. I only have about two months left before I take the veil."

Then—either unconcerned or wholly unaware of her effect on him—she walked around him, sauntered back through his garden terrace, and melted off into the night.

And she didn't look back.

Not even once.

He knew because he watched her the whole way, until there was only night where she had been, and he was all alone on his cliff top with nothing save the wind.

CHAPTER FOUR

TWO NIGHTS LATER, Brita was sitting at one of her favorite viewpoints. It was high on a rocky outcropping in the hills, far away from the tangle of the touristy villages down below. She liked to sit there most nights, but especially on nights like this one, when she could watch the moon rise over the sea.

The wolf pup she'd saved from a trap the previous winter sat next to her, panting slightly. She called him Heracles, and he whined when she glanced at him, leaning his shoulder against her legs.

Heracles wouldn't let her pet him, proud wolf that he was, but if she sat still enough he would sometimes lean in to show his affection.

She was going to miss this.

For many reasons, but foremost among them the fact she hadn't seen any kind of physical affection in the convent. The sisters prayed. They sang. They cooked food together and ate it together. But in the three years she'd spent there, studying them and their ways, no one had ever leaned in the way this mighty wolf was now.

It was only the creatures she'd spent so much time with who ever had.

The closer it got to the end of her year of temptation, the more bittersweet it all felt. Because so much would be different when she was back in the convent. As supportive as the sisters were about her ideas for a wildlife refuge, and as comforting as she found a sedate life with a predictable routine, it wasn't as if the sisters were going to take to wolf cubs galloping about the convent. Or any of the other creatures that liked to follow Brita about and, sometimes, lean in for a bit of comfort and communion.

You are just like a raggedy, uncouth Snow White, her stepmother had once sneered over an empty bottle of whatever she'd been necking that night.

Brita had taken that as a compliment. *Did you know*, she'd replied, *that animals are far better judges of character than we humans are? They can sense bad intentions from kilometers away. And they never suffer fools*.

She had been sent to her room without any food that day, though sadly it had been Maria's day off, and she still thought it was worth it.

That was life, wasn't it? The peace in the convent came at a price.

Everything did.

That was the one lesson her family had taught her that she had taken to heart, because she knew too well it was true.

"But who ever told you that life was designed to make you happy?" she asked in a low sort of voice, halfway to a croon so that Heracles made a low noise in response.

He was a talker. Between him and the moon and the sea, who could be lonely?

"Why should you not be happy?" came another voice.

From behind her.

But Brita recognized it instantly.

Maybe it was more accurate to say that her body responded to it instantly, the way it had done every time she'd thought of him since that first night.

And, for some reason, she had thought about the so-called Monster of the Mediterranean *a lot*.

He had interrupted her sleep. He had given her twisty, dark, aching dreams that haunted her, though they made no sense. They left her wide-awake with too many *feelings* pouring all over her and through her like honey, her body flushed and sensitive and *heavy*—

Brita had been certain she must be ill. Though none of the usual remedies she employed seemed to help.

Heracles growled softly, then loped off. She knew he was finding a new vantage point, where he would stay and watch over her from afar. That was what he did.

And Brita didn't *need* to turn to see who it was who stood some distance away from her on this particular hilltop, but she did anyway. Because, something in her admitted softly, she *wanted* to look at him. How bizarre was that?

Why should the very notion of looking at the man make her feel a rush of that strange sickness all over again?

The first time she'd seen him, he had looked as she expected a man like him would. He'd worn the typical rich man's dark, bespoke suit in a fabric that seemed to hug his body in ways her father's attire thankfully never did. It should have seemed formal and odd, but he had somehow made it seem almost casual.

Or perhaps it had been that he exuded a certain confidence that made it clear that he was as at his ease when strolling into a stranger's kitchen as he was standing out on his personal cliff top. *He* was at ease wherever he went, his whole *person* seemed to whisper, and Brita understood this without having to ask.

In that way, this man was not so different from a wolf.

Though Heracles had never made her feel so inordinately feverish.

Tonight Asterion Teras was dressed in truly casual clothes. He wore a pair of trousers that she hadn't heard from afar, which suggested they were made of a fabric both soft and likely dear. And worse by far for her equanimity, he was wearing a T-shirt.

Brita could not recall ever having a reaction to a *T-shirt* before. She never paid much attention to men and the things they wore. They were not animals who needed her, so unless they were actively repulsive to her—the ones who *gaped* at her, or encouraged her to *smile,* or became irate if she did not respond to them, or wished to marry her at her father's command—she did not see them. She must have been presented with a great number of T-shirts before in her lifetime, particularly as she lived on an island filled with tourists decked out in holiday gear, but it was a shocking truth that she couldn't remember a single one. Not one like this. Not one like *his.*

This T-shirt looked like marble in the moonlight, a sculptural feat.

Brita had seen statues in museums just as she had seen members of her family around the sunken, abandoned pool that hadn't held any water aside from rain in as long as she could remember. She had always thought privately that men's bodies were a bit boring, really, for all they strutted about like pigeons.

But tonight it was as if the sight of him sent her into anaphylactic shock.

Everything was tight. She felt…red. She itched everywhere.

Maybe that explained all this. Maybe this was an *allergy.*

"How did you find me?" she asked, because she was the one who tracked creatures through the hills of this island. He was the one who lived in that marvelously seductive house that had seemed more a dream the cliffside had than any sort of dwelling place. It suggested he was far more wild and starkly uncivilized than she would have imagined a member of the Teras family could be, if she'd thought about it.

Until that night, she had not thought about it. Not

really. She had seen the place from afar during her travels, a strange tangle of glass and light and steel that seemed to weave its way into the cliff itself, as if it was an organic thing when it was plainly not. Some nights it gleamed in the distance and she'd had the stray thought that it seemed *alive*.

It had been different up close. The house had seemed elemental.

Maybe he had, too, though that hardly made sense.

"Everyone knows where to look for the goddess of the hunt when the moon rises," he was saying.

Her heart was beating so hard it didn't occur to her to question that, for it wasn't really an answer at all.

"What did you ask me—about happiness?" she asked instead, though she knew. She remembered. *Why should you not be happy?*

It made her feel unsteady, that question. It felt like a detonation, one that kept on and on. One that was even worse than the allergic reaction she was currently suffering through.

He was looking at her almost curiously. Almost, but not quite—there was something deeper there. Darker, maybe. "Isn't that what you said to your dog?"

Brita looked back reflexively, and though she couldn't find the glint of Heracles's eyes in the dark, she knew he was there. She didn't correct Asterion. Wolves were like anything else, she had found. If people wanted to believe they didn't exist, nothing she could say or do could convince them. And it didn't make them any less real. Or any less dangerous.

She couldn't make sense of why her skin prickled the way it did then, instantly covered in too many goose bumps to count, when all she did was look back at Asterion.

"Why do they call you a monster?" she asked him. "As far as I can tell, all you seem to do is worry about lost creatures and moon rises."

"I think you have you and me confused, little huntress."

Something about his cultured voice, with that undercurrent of something rougher, deeper, seemed to abrade her skin where it was already so desperately prickly. She told herself it was allergies again, nothing more. Or those words, *little huntress,* in his mouth like that.

It was a strange thing for a man to say. Especially if he said it like that.

He moved out from the shadows that marked the edge of the trees. Then he came out until he could stand beside her, there in a small clearing that she had long considered her own, for no one else ever ventured here. It should have felt a violation to have him here. To have *anyone* here, she corrected herself, because these were her hills, her views. This was where she came to *escape* people, not entertain them, though no one had ever tested that before. For who else dared trek out this far, through so much dense vegetation, to see a pretty view on an island that had so many?

Yet she did not feel violated in the least when he came to stand beside her. Instead, she realized with a start that some of the dreams she'd been having had been whispering little memories to her all along.

Like the scent of him. She hadn't imagined it. It had been there in the air that night.

It hadn't been that strange sensation in her belly that she'd attributed to standing at the edge of a steep cliff.

It was *him*.

A hint of something like woodsmoke, something brighter woven into it, and a kind of heat she did not understand, but knew was simply him.

She drifted closer and somehow held back from sniffing him the way the wolves did.

For even she knew that was not acceptable behavior.

And besides, it was likely to make her allergies even worse.

"You told me I could call you," he said in that voice again, his gaze out on the moon and the ladder it made across the surface of the sea as it lazily considered rising. "I thought this would be the next best thing."

Brita knew she gave the impression of having, perhaps, been raised by the wolves she liked so much. In some ways, being raised by any of her creatures would have been an improvement over her situation. But she had, in fact, interacted with humans before Asterion. Even she knew that as far as explanations went, this was a bad one.

Yet she couldn't quite bring herself to mind.

"If you've come to tell me that you found something crying again, I'm afraid you've made a bit of a miscalculation," she told him, and though she did not allow herself to look at the T-shirt, she was aware of it. She was *fully* aware of it. "In future, it's better to stay near the wounded thing so it doesn't run off. It is likely to be gone again, like last time."

When he turned his head, she found herself caught as surely as if he had trapped her that way, or possibly between the span of his palms. "My mistake."

And it seemed to cost her something to turn her head back to the moon, the beckoning sea. It seemed to take her too long to stop feeling her breath all the way in, then out. A little too quick, a little too rough.

She expected something to happen. He seemed the type to make his own weather wherever he went, and she braced for it, for surely a man like this did not simply decide to take a remote hike only to exchange a few words. No one ever had before.

Instead, he stood there beside her, his scent a part of the view, the breeze. The trees at her back, the sea stretching out before them both.

They must have stood there a long time.

But after a while, the moon was high and Brita started to feel itchy again. Feverish. She needed to find a place to camp tonight, and perhaps make herself a poultice from the herbs she foraged as she walked. For the allergies.

She turned and headed back for the trail, the one she'd made herself with her own two feet, and it seemed the most natural thing in the world for him to fall into place beside her, matching his stride to hers.

It felt almost comfortable.

The truth was, Brita did not know a great deal about comfort.

"You can't possibly be committed to your own happiness," she said, aware when he slanted a look in her direction that she'd done that thing she did again. The sisters at the nunnery had explained with great patience that not everyone lived inside her head, and she had to engage in conversation if she wished everyone to know what she was talking about at any given time.

A far kinder approach to that habit of hers, the one she'd developed as a child who spent most of her time inside that head of hers, than the one her family had employed.

But he didn't seem lost. "Can't I?"

"Your brother is the happy-go-lucky one. Too charming to live, they say. His smile could make the Mediterranean dim beside him, according to all reports. And of course, you could look just like him if you wanted, could you not?"

"Our features are identical," he said, which, again, was not exactly an answer to the question she'd asked.

"I only mean that you could be just as bright and shiny if you wished. You clearly don't."

"Does it follow then, that I am therefore forever in the depths of despair?"

She danced over the exposed roots in her way, and let herself swing out a bit off the trail, using the trunk of a young tree to hold her. She wasn't sure why the look on his face was…slightly arrested as she came back to earth.

Or why there was a response inside of her, like a song.

Not a feverish one at all.

"I don't know. Are you in the depths of despair?" Something about *how* he was silent had her hurrying on, suddenly worried that it was possible that he actually was, and she sensed somehow that he wouldn't welcome it if she paused to dig into it. To him. "Maybe you confine all your happiness to places where you can be sure you're in private. That's fair enough. But surely you must know that outside of those places, you are thought of as the grim one."

"We cannot all be my brother, bestowing his charms as freely as he does, to all and sundry." Brita had heard the tales of the great rivalry between the brothers, but Asterion did not sound the way her father did when he discussed those he considered his rivals. Peevish and dark and vengeful. Asterion sounded almost…fond. "Or even my grandmother, who commands a certain kind of attention wherever she goes, and caters to it."

"I've never seen the point of attempting to be someone else," Brita told him matter-of-factly. "And I have been given many opportunities to do exactly that. My cousin Panagiota is five years older than me, and according to my family, possesses every virtue that I do not. Save one."

She looked beside her and he was watching her intently, a terrific way to tumble down the side of the mountain. She nearly told him so, but in her experience, men did not like it when presented with facts they might have overlooked. So she kept that particular fact to herself and supposed she would have to do her best to catch him.

"Why should it matter which one of you is the more virtuous?" he asked.

"It doesn't matter to me." Brita laughed. "But as my father likes to say, usually quite loudly, it's Panagiota who has a face for the nunnery. And me, his cursed daughter, who longs for the nunnery when I have a face that would make Helen of Troy herself jealous."

They walked on, and through a tricky bit, where the trail strayed a bit too close to some hillside erosion. Brita was on alert, but somehow, this expensive man in his *T-shirt* seemed as fleet-footed as a mountain goat.

"I have never heard a woman discuss her own beauty in such a fashion," he said after some while had passed. "It is disarming."

And yet, somehow, Brita knew that was a lie. She thought there was very little that could disarm this man. And very little that ever had.

Besides, her beauty was an inescapable fact. A fact that seemed to matter to everyone who laid eyes on her, though it had never mattered to her.

But she focused on the conversation they were actually having instead of the various streams of thought in her head. The sisters would be so proud. "My family tells me I am distressingly unfeminine.

By that they mean that I ought to blush and stammer and pretend I have imposter syndrome, when I have a mirror as well as anyone else. And it's not as if being in possession of this face has ever done me any good. If I'd inherited the same features as the rest of the women in my family, I would have been left to my own devices long ago. I would not need to join a convent. I could simply do as I liked."

"And what is that, Brita?"

He stopped walking then, turning to look at her. The breeze was sighing through the trees. The moonlight filtered down, dancing through the tree branches, making it all feel like some kind of a dream.

Maybe it was. It was a lot like the dreams she'd been having lately, achy and hot.

"What do I want?" When he gazed back at her, clearly encouraging her to continue, she swallowed. "I want what everyone wants. It is not so special."

"Humor me."

"I want to do what I have always done." And when she flushed then, it was a different wash of color, a different kind of heat. It was half temper and half the little bit of shame her family had managed to put on her despite her best efforts to ignore them entirely. "I want to take care of creatures more helpless than myself. It's not even particularly odd. There are veterinarians the world over. Wildlife specialists. The world is filled these days with more compassionate advocates for animals than not. Did you know that this island has a vast number of indigenous species, some of which can only been found here? On this island only, out of all the islands in the Mediterranean. Apparently this has never interested the crown overmuch, but it interests me."

And, as ever, there was only the sound of her fervent words, hanging there between them. When Brita knew better than that. She'd learned that no one wished to know what she actually thought about anything. Even when—especially when—they asked.

"There are other wildlife advocates here," he said after a moment, a stunned sort of look in his eyes. Usually people she was actually passionate in front of demanded apologies, and Brita understood then that something in her would crack into pieces if he turned out to be the sort of person who needed her apologies. But he didn't. He kept on. "As I told you before, I was required to consult with a number of them when I chose to build a house that some thought disturbed the habitat of native species."

"Yes, and they are marvelous, these advocates," she said. "But I would like there to be an actual wildlife refuge here. Where we could rehabilitate animals in need, release them back into the wild if possible, and if not, let them live out the rest of their days without having to worry about scaring a tourist and being killed for the insult. And I don't need you to tell me that I'm overly emotionally invested," she said quickly, before he could. Because everyone did. "I know I am. My family tells me so all the time. Luckily, once I become a nun in full, the sisters have pledged their support. It might not be the kind of refuge I imagine, but there's no reason why we can't do something." She blew out a breath. "Smaller scale means just what it says. Smaller. Not *less than*."

"Did someone tell you that?"

She smiled at him then, though she could not have said why. "The Abbess. A great many times. Maybe someday it will take."

"You seem resigned to your fate, little huntress."

"I like the convent," she said. He started walking again, and there was a pleasure in it, she found. Matching the way her body moved to the way his did, as if it was a kind of dance, to pick their way down the side of the hill very few ever climbed in the first place. "I was raised in a lot of chaos. A lot of turmoil, I suppose."

And something in her chest seemed to stutter at the look on his face then. As if he knew the kind of chaos and turmoil she would have thought his wealth protected him from. She cautioned herself against reading too much into a look on a man's face in the middle of so many trees doing their best to block out the moonlight.

Still, she wondered.

Yet she continued. "Every day in the convent is the same. The same prayers, the same schedule. The seasons change, as much as they ever do here, but little else does. It feels eternal. Safe. I like that."

She felt the curve of his lips before she looked over to see it. "Surely, Brita, if you're called to a holy life, you must mention your own holiness first. Isn't that the point of it all?"

Bria thought it was such an intimate thing, to walk beside another, surrounded by only dark, trees and all the creatures who lived here. Such an intimate thing to nearly feel the brush of his arm. To feel as if, were he to look at her again, she might so easily stumble and fall all the way down to the bottom of the hill and hardly care at all.

"I think that it is too easy for too many people to confuse things." She found the moon in the sky, though it did not penetrate the trees as well here as before. Still, she knew it was there. "There is very little in this world that is not sacred, if you stop and let it in. And it is not my holiness that I'm seeking. What I'm seeking is a life of service."

A life of *meaning,* she did not say. She knew better than that. Her father had howled with laughter the one time she'd dared say that aloud.

Think of what you can mean to your family, and be still, her stepmother had said waspishly.

While Brita had vowed that she would never waste her life as a bauble on a rich man's arm. No matter what she had to do to avoid it.

She thought that Asterion would pepper her with more questions, because people always did. How could she give up this or that or the other thing—but he didn't ask.

Instead, they walked. In a hushed silence that reminded her of morning prayers. That sacred. That intimate. When they got down to the bottom of the hill, she saw another sports car haphazardly parked beneath the olive trees. She saw the way the olive leaves glinted as silver as the moon, as if they were made as much of moonlight as anything else.

As much moonlight as she could feel inside her, even now.

"I'll call you soon," he told her, and when he moved toward her, she couldn't really say what she thought he was doing, but everything in her surged forward, and upward, and outward, almost as if she wanted—

Yet all he did was brush his thumb over one cheekbone.

She wondered if perhaps one of the overhanging tree branches had brushed her as they walked, if he simply meant to wipe the mark it had left away. It was that quick, that glancing.

Yet they both stood there for a long moment, as if something had changed.

As if in the space between them, now, in the wake of that touch, something had kindled.

And long after his car had disappeared down the winding lane, Brita stayed where he'd left her, staring up at the moon that had witnessed all this.

One hand pressed her cheek, as if he was the one who'd left a mark.

CHAPTER FIVE

"YOUR FAITH IN my abilities is overwhelming, truly," Asterion said dryly, some days later.

But his grandmother was unmoved.

She had summoned him before her yet again, so she could sit on her throne, pretend it was a real one, and wave her elegant hands around as if, were they both to concentrate more fully, they could both see a queenly scepter there. He suspected she did not need to focus at all to envision it.

"I'm not sure what faith would do for me," Dimitra replied in her usual tart way. "I have seen no evidence that you have even approached the girl I chose for you."

"I beg your pardon. I was unaware that you wanted to tag along like some kind of chaperone. Or do I mean a third wheel?"

And he could have told her that, in fact, he had taken to skulking about the hills in order to meet up with the half-wild creature she'd decreed would be his, but he didn't. He told himself that there was no sense in talking about negotiations until they were done. That was sound business strategy, nothing more.

Though there was something in him that wondered if it was something else. An urge to keep what happened between him and Brita private...

But Asterion dismissed that almost as soon as he thought it. He was not sentimental. He had seen where that sort of thing led and had arranged his life to prevent it. One strange girl could hardly change the habits of a lifetime.

Even sitting in this house brought it back. The shouting from afar, the sounds of splintering glass and sobs. Muffled accusations being thrown with abandon and then, worse, the ones he could hear.

His parents always waved these things away as if they were nothing.

We are passionate, he had heard his father say once, as if that was an excuse.

Asterion did not allow himself to wonder if he would make the same excuse if he'd lived through the accident.

What he did know was that he would never put himself in a position where he would need to make such an excuse himself. To anyone.

He eyed his grandmother and her hand-waving with more stern grimness than he might have, had he not been forced to consider *sentiment* and the worst night of his life in the midst of what should have been a perfectly rational business discussion. "Information that might have been useful, Yia Yia, would have included things like where to actually locate the woman you proclaimed I was to claim as my own. Instead, I was forced to track down a host of rumors and innuendo concerning her. She might not be the typical heiress but nor is she, as I have been led to believe, a huntress of old, stalking the hills of the island to harvest men's souls."

His grandmother's eyes glittered. "You seem very certain of that, dear child."

This was a game, he knew. And Asterion had always been fantastic at games. What were games but another way to practice winning? He had always been exceptionally good at winning.

He felt he was winning now, in fact, but part of that involved keeping the state of affairs, such as it was, to himself. Not only because it would annoy his grandmother, which he felt she had coming to her. But because it made sense to play his cards close to the vest until he had news to share that would make the indisputable fact that he was beating Dimitra at her own game clear.

This was why he did not respond to her the way she likely expected. Instead, he lounged across from her on one of her baroque couches that offended his stark sense of style in every regard—which she knew very well—and only gazed back at her. As close to *idly* as he ever got. "What do you know about the Martis family?"

"The family?" Dimitra let out a sharp bark that was not quite a laugh. "I know too much and none of it precisely awash in glory. The girl's grandfather made quite a name for himself when I was young.

He cut a swathe through the local population until he was finally forced to marry by royal decree. At which point he was even more shocking." She gazed off as if into the past, tapping her fingers against her chin. "Brita's father was the oldest son of that unhappy union and has always been particularly unappealing. I have never been quite sure how he ended up married. Twice, no less. The family has been stampeding through the remains of a very old fortune for generations and rejoiced when it became clear that nature had been so kind to Brita."

Her gaze was canny then, as if waiting for Asterion to acknowledge Brita's stunning beauty. He only gazed at her, impassive, until she smiled as if he'd admitted far more than that.

She sounded far too smug when she continued. "They would very much like to marry her off to a man of means, the better to raise the family profile and pay off debt."

It was nothing Asterion didn't know, but he was surprised all the same that she said it out loud. "And you imagine that I am the appropriate man for the job?" He shook his head. "I always thought that your innate snobbery and obsession with the family legacy would inure me forever from fortune hunters of any description."

"Don't be tiresome, child." Dimitra sat a bit straighter in her makeshift throne. "The Martis family is many things, most of them admittedly squalid, but no one can deny the bloodline is one of the oldest and most noble on the island. I have never given

Vasilis Martis the time of day, nor acknowledged the existence of his egregious upstart of a wife, and can imagine no reason I ever shall. But that does not change the bloodline. I've done you a favor, Asterion. Brita is all that is innocent and good. She wishes to become a *nun* in this age of astonishing bad behavior and excessive internet nonsense. For all her scampering about the hills, it is quite obvious that she is not only pure and untouched, but somehow otherworldly. And, as it has perhaps escaped your notice, she is the most beautiful woman on this island. You're welcome."

Only because this was his beloved grandmother did he keep to himself his distaste at hearing her discuss Brita as if she was nothing more than a piece of meat hanging in a butcher shop.

"That is great deal of information," he said. "I cannot imagine what made you think you should send me off without sharing it all in the first place. What I don't understand is how she even came to your notice."

"I have my methods." She smiled benignly, when she was nothing of the kind. "Especially when it comes to the production of beautiful great-grandchildren. Why all these questions? Do you find yourself overset by the task before you?"

He had always known that it was his duty to produce children. To provide Dimitra, and even himself, with heirs to all of this. And he had always assumed that, come the day, he would approach the making of them with the cold logic that had defined his life.

Yet thinking of making babies with Brita made him feel as if all the air had gone out of the room.

Because the making of babies turned into the raising of children, and he knew one thing well. He would not repcat his parents' mistakes. Even if that meant he would need to remove himself completely from his children's lives.

Better that than the alternative.

But he had no intention of letting his grandmother see him worried. He refused to call it worry. He smirked. "Now you insult me, Yia Yia."

Asterion left her after some more affectionate sparring and drove back down her personal hillside to find himself inching through the usual traffic in the seaside villages on the lone coastal road. Here, everyone recognized him and either nodded with respect or turned pale with fright, as was his due. He had earned these reactions. He cherished them. He was not his parents, who had lost sight of their reputations in the heat of their endless love affair and the tempest of it that had consumed them both. And nearly taken Asterion and Poseidon along with them—

But he did not like to think of the accident. It did him no good.

Though he supposed he could understand why his grandmother felt she had no choice but to act in such a typically Teras manner, strong-arming her remaining relatives into expanding the family while she was still around to see it. She had lost more than anyone that night.

He did not appreciate that it had led her here, but he could understand why it had.

Still, he found himself thinking—though he would fling himself from his own cliff before admitting to such a thing, especially to his grandmother—that this was all a little more…unexpectedly difficult than he'd imagined.

Not seeking Brita out, or spending time with her. That was not difficult at all. That was the problem.

He had not expected to *like* her.

Asterion hit a button on his phone and rang his brother in London, who answered on the first ring.

"Not exactly the best time, brother," Poseidon drawled, though if that were true, he would not have picked up the call.

"You like everyone," he said. "Too much, one might say."

"Everyone does say that. Particularly you. With alarming regularity."

Asterion stopped for yet another pack of holidaymakers who streamed across the road, blinded to anything but the beckoning Mediterranean before them. There were people everywhere on a bright day like this, everything a riot of color against the whitewashed walls that were considered a hallmark of this part of the world.

He glared at the tourists. "I find it difficult to understand how a person moves through life, deliberately immersing himself in the company of so many."

There was a rustling bit of noise on the other end of the line. He thought perhaps he heard his brother murmur something, no doubt to one of his many conquests.

But when Poseidon spoke into the phone again, there was no other sound at all. "What exactly are you asking me?"

"I regret the impulse."

"Are you..." His twin sounded delighted. "Are you asking me to teach you how to be charming?"

"I am not." He thought of the look on Brita's face when he'd touched her cheek that first time. Just a brush. Hardly a touch at all. And yet it lived in him still. "I merely wondered what the appeal was. As I have lately heard that I am known as *the grim one*."

"Were you under the impression that you were known as something else?" Poseidon laughed. "Because that would likely require that you stop acting as if you are Atlas himself, hefting the globe on your shoulders at every opportunity and making certain to look aggrieved while you do it."

"I am a man of some intensity," Asterion acknowledged, and he wasn't certain that he liked that he was having this conversation at all. Was this that *self-doubt* he heard so much about from people he did not hire? Or worse, the newly bandied about *imposter syndrome*, which he had never experienced in his life, because he was Asterion Teras and he deserved every single thing that was his and more. "You of all people should understand that it does not make me—"

"The Monster of the Mediterranean?" Poseidon laughed again. "But you are so good at it. You snarl about, dark and brooding, and the poor besotted girls flock to you all the same."

"I suppose I wondered why you bother to charm them at all when I am living proof that there is no need."

"I prefer honey to vinegar, brother," Poseidon said, and unlike their grandmother, Poseidon had at least committed himself to the study of honey. He was famous for it. "Try it. You might discover a whole side of yourself you never knew was there."

"If that is a recommendation—"

"I would never dream of making such recommendations." Poseidon's voice was dry. "After all there's nothing you don't know, as eldest brother of all of one minute. Think of all that you have learned in those sixty seconds you graced this earth without me. What could I possibly have to tell you?"

"I regret that I called," Asterion said darkly, which only set his brother to laughing even more.

He had that ringing in his ears even after he ended the call. And as he navigated his way out of the tourist centers of the beachside villages, heading back into the hills and following the road that curved around and around and eventually became his drive. Once again, he felt unsettled.

Once again, he disliked it. Intensely.

Ever since he had laid eyes on Brita Martis, Asterion had not been...himself. Not quite.

He decided as he drove that it was because he was forced to play this part.

Wooing anyone, a woman or a client or a deal, was

not in his nature. Asterion had never been the sort to sell himself. He had never needed to. His reputation preceded him wherever he went and did most of the work for him. Before he had built his own reputation, he'd had his family's.

He had never been the sort to hang about, having pointless conversations with anyone, much less a woman. He had never *walked in the moonlight* without some other, better purpose. There were often women hanging about him, and he indulged himself as he pleased. He was a man of certain means and a great many skills, and he liked a woman who could meet him in all things. Stamina. Imagination.

But most important, he kept his indulgences to the dark hours and did not wish to think of anyone when he woke.

And because he did not wish it, he did not. Such was the iron and steel of his self-control.

It had been his compass all these years.

That was the worst part about this Brita situation. She haunted him. Here it was full daylight, he hadn't even tasted her, and he was thinking about her when he had whole empires to run. It was madness.

He detested it—and yet he could not stop.

Once at his house, he strode down the stairs that led him along the spine of the house so he could make his way to the part set aside for business. His refuge. This was where he had made certain that in one sense, the Teras legacy would last forever. He sat at his desk of stone, built into the cliffside, and yet he could not seem to focus his thoughts as usual.

He had built this house from the depths of his own imagination, had laid many of the stones with his own hands. He had built it to his precise specifications, so this office was deep in the hillside on one end and yet offered an expansive view of the sea on the other, with a wide terrace above the crashing waves where he often took calls.

Usually the only thing he thought of in this space was work.

Yet even now she haunted him.

Even here, he could not escape.

His compass was broken. He blamed her—but he shut that down before it could take root, as it tasted suspiciously like emotion. Passion. These things that were anathema to him.

And grimly—yes, *grimly*—he set himself to the pile of tasks that awaited him anyway.

When night fell, he gave up and took the stairs again, this time back up to his gardens that sprawled out to the edge of the cliff. He considered, then dismissed, the idea of a hard swim in his eternity pool. For there was only one way he truly wished to use his body tonight and it was not available to him.

Because the thought of another woman would not do. He wanted her.

He wanted *her* and that was a disaster.

But when he turned back toward the house, she was there. On the edge of the trees, watching him like a ghost.

Asterion wished he could pretend she was a figment of his imagination, the one he had been unaware he possessed before now, but he could not. She was all too real.

He could *feel* her, from the soles of his feet to his sex to that pounding mess where his heart should have been.

And he knew that this was supposed to be a wooing, not the kind of hard, dark wanting he excelled in. He knew that his grandmother was right. Brita was untried, untouched. An innocent in all ways—

Yet as he drew closer to her, he couldn't find the words to cut this tension inside him. To change that driving need, deep in his blood.

"Asterion," she began as he approached.

But he couldn't help himself. Perhaps he did not wish to help himself, not when there was this unbearable *wanting* that made everything before her seem pale, insubstantial, even something closer to sad.

He moved closer, took her face in his hands, and kissed her.

At last, he kissed her.

Once, then again, Asterion fit his lips to hers, he tasted her heat, and he kissed her even deeper.

Until, to his delight, she kissed him back.

It was like getting sucked into an undertow, a tumble so intense, so overwhelming, that he might have considered it too much to bear if it hadn't also been so deliriously *good*.

Her mouth beneath his was artless. She tasted faintly of herbs and made him think of cool waterfalls and rich, warm Mediterranean nights.

Asterion did not permit himself escapes of any

kind that involved women, not work, but Brita tempted him to do more than simply lose his head. She tasted like heat and destiny. She would lead him straight into the kind of oblivion he would never be able to shake, or live without. The kind that could topple great men, raze cities, upend the world no matter whose shoulders it rested upon—

The kind that had killed his parents.

He set her away from him abruptly, though not without the strangest sort of...*tenderness*. He could feel it all over him. In him.

For her.

As if being near this woman made him someone he did not know.

For a moment there was only the tangle of their breath, there in the night, with the trees keeping watch all around them. He could see the gleam of her gaze, gold and silver, sun and moon, twisting around and around inside him, and luring him closer. Luring him—

But this was not the plan. This was not how he intended for this project of his grandmother's to go, and this was certainly not how he permitted himself to behave. Not ever. Asterion was a man of sober contemplation and swift, decisive action.

He did not lose his head. In the moonlight or anywhere else.

He took a step back, and when that did not break the spell, he stepped back again.

Yet the distance did nothing to help. Even then, he was far too taken with her. He was far too...*pos-*

sessed, something in him whispered, when that could not be possible.

Because he was a man who had turned his back on anything that even hinted of strong emotion, or anything else he could not control, since the day he had lost most of his family and nearly himself to boot.

He would not allow himself to stray from the standards of behavior he'd set for himself then.

He had never strayed in all this time.

That he was debating this as he stood here, staring at her, sent something in him spinning madly like he was no more than a drunk. When he did not allow himself the mess and muddle of intoxication.

But then that same sensation seemed to *tighten* as if his ribs were closing in on him.

He turned abruptly and stalked back the way he'd come, hardly aware of the ground beneath his feet, so desperate was he to simply get away. To disappear. To put space between him and this woman who was supposed to be an exercise. A challenge.

A game, at best.

Because games were easy for Asterion. He won them without even trying.

He did not understand what this was. What *she* was—

But he stopped short when something *thunked* into the tree directly in front of him, there in the last line of trees keeping him out of sight of his house.

Asterion glared balefully at the arrow that shook there, wobbling slightly in the tree trunk only centimeters from his head.

Scant centimeters at that.

He turned, very slowly, and even though there could only be one explanation, and therefore only one possible image before him—he still couldn't believe it when he saw it. When he saw *her*.

He couldn't make sense of Brita standing there before him, the bow that was normally slung over her back in her hands, drawn back with another arrow notched into place and set to fly.

This time, he suspected she would not miss.

"You shot at me."

It was not a question. It was indignation, pure and simple.

Affront, crystallized now, when he could still taste her on his tongue.

"What was *that?*" she demanded.

"A kiss," he gritted out.

He reached over and wrapped his fingers around the arrow in the tree beside him, his eyes still on Brita, and those two things seem to fuse together inside of him, filling him with a nearly unbearable heat.

Asterion had never felt anything like it.

He told himself it was fury, nothing more, but he didn't quite believe it.

"That was not a kiss," she corrected him, and she was frowning, which should have marred the peerless beauty of her face.

It did not.

If anything, it made her look less like a perfect statue and more like a woman. A flesh and blood woman, that was. Not an object to worship from afar, but a warm, hot human woman who would rub against him, clamp him between her thighs, and ride him until they both cracked wide-open, entrenching him in her soft heat all the while.

God help him, he was as hard as a pike, like the shaft of the arrow he gripped in his hand.

He wrenched it out of the tree trunk and looked down at it. He couldn't think of the last time he'd seen an actual arrow. Much less one with a matching bow. And certainly it had never occurred to him, even in his wildest childhood games with his brother, that anyone would ever dare *aim one at his head*.

"I think, little huntress, that the tales are true. You are untouched."

"Obviously I'm not untouched. For you have touched me."

"And what happens now?" he demanded, though somehow, the affront and indignation had faded. Now the only thing left was that heat. And the blazing thing between them, more gold and silver than even her gaze, seemed to hum in them both. "Will you strike me down for my temerity? Are you so beholden to your own innocence, Brita? That is how those old stories go, is it not? A virgin huntress is beloved by the moon while she remains pure, then is thrust into the unforgiving daylight when she falls into the earthly clutches of unworthy men."

"I think you'll find that's a parable for the fate of all women, in one way or another," Brita said dryly.

"That would make me unworthy." Asterion bared

his teeth, though he would not call it a smile. "And I confess to you that I am a great many insalubrious things where women are concerned, but never that."

He couldn't tell if she drifted closer or he did, or maybe they both moved, but when they were nearer to each other, she lowered that bow. And he watched, his own tension growing within him, as she let the tension in the bow go, too.

Her whole body moved with the force of the breath she took in, then blew out.

"I don't understand," she said quietly, her eyes darker than before. "I thought a kiss was supposed to be a little bauble of a thing. Something gleaming and bright, a sweet joy in the moment, and then quickly forgotten. Not...*that*."

He watched her face in the moonlight, able to see the way she trembled—just slightly—and there was no small part of him that exulted in that. And not only because it felt like winning.

But also because that meant that he was not the only one who had spun so far out in all that sensation.

At least there was that.

"Ever since I met you I've felt sick," she said, and he almost laughed, so far was that from his own thoughts. But she was frowning in that ferocious way of hers, and she moved closer to him as she spoke, still gripping her bow, but thankfully pointing the arrow at the ground between them. "Terrible fevers. Aches. And itching, everywhere. I keep thinking I am falling ill, but I never quite fall and it's worse when you are near." Her frown deepened. "But better, too, and then that kiss—"

"I see."

And he did. That odd tenderness washed over him again, but he didn't interrogate it. He reached over and traced an intricate little pattern over her mouth, her full lips with the top one suggesting the perfect bow. To match the one she carried, he supposed. This time, he watched as goose bumps broke out all over her skin, her eyes flashed, and sure enough, a flush rose up all over her lovely cheeks.

Not a fever.

But he knew the cure.

And better still, he knew full well that there was no emotion necessary. Only pleasure.

For the first time since meeting Brita and reeling from his response to her, he felt like himself again. There was no reason to think that this was anything but attraction, and he knew how to handle that.

He knew, at last, how to handle her.

"Good news," he told her then, and no longer minded that he ached, too. "You are not ill, little huntress."

Her lips parted. "What is it then?"

Asterion shifted his weight backward and uncurled his clenched fist, looking down at the arrow. And it took him entirely too long to order the mess of thoughts and the muddle of sensation inside him.

But as he did, the answer became clear. He thought of the things his grandmother had told him. About her family, and her history. He thought of what little he'd seen of that family with his own eyes, shrieking at each other into the night.

Those were reasonable, practical considerations.

And they had nothing to do with the decision he made. He only knew that he could not woo this woman. Not when he wanted her so badly.

Not when she wanted him, too.

Asterion understood that the sooner they burned off this attraction between them, the better things would be. He could control it that way. He could make this work.

But now he looked up from that arrow she'd shot at him and into those eyes of hers, gold and silver, now mixed with wonder.

"It is simple, Brita." He even felt himself smile, slightly, as he said it. A real smile this time. As if he didn't have to pretend to be someone else. As if he wasn't the Monster of the Mediterranean at all, and that should have scared him. That should have made him wish that the arrow in his hand had pierced him straight through. Then again, maybe it had, but he was the one holding it now. "You will have to marry me."

CHAPTER SIX

BRITA DIDN'T MEAN to let out a sigh, but it escaped anyway. She had thought for a moment there that he was about to say something magical, but instead it was this.

The same old bore, and after there had been *kissing*.

It seemed unfair. And right when she'd started to think he was something a bit more thrilling than an *allergy*.

"Once again, that's really very disappointing," she said, after too many moments slid past. During which she was forced to admit to herself that she had not come here in a selfless desire to search for an animal in need. She'd known it the moment she'd seen him.

Brita had come here for this. For him.

And there was something shocking about the way he laughed then. Not only because she was sure that she had heard that he'd never done so in all his days. That he was nothing but a shroud of grim intensity and that all the laughter and smiles were his brother's.

But because his laughter seemed to *ignite* inside her own skin.

"A disappointment?" That word seemed to set him off again, because he laughed more, and it was a dark, rusty sort of sound that seemed to twine its way deep into her bones. "Me? Are you certain?"

"Everyone wants to marry me," she said, scowling at him. "And every time, the notion is presented to me as if it is not only the first time it has ever been mentioned, but is a gift. Something that should make me fall to my knees in praise and pleasure."

He wiped at his face as if his own laughter had made his eyes water. "If you feel moved, do not let me stop you."

She unnotched her arrow from her bow and slid it back into her sheath, then tossed her bow over her shoulder, too.

"When I was at university, all I ever heard the other girls talk about was how little men wished to marry. How they all had to be hunted down like wild game, lured into elaborate traps, and tricked into taking part in the whole enterprise. I have not found this to be so."

"Then you and I are alike," he told her. "For I, too, have received more marriage proposals than I could possibly count."

That made even less sense. Brita puffed out an annoyed sort of laugh herself. "Then you know how annoying they are."

"But I had never offered anyone a proposal my-self," he continued in that dark, inexorable way, and suddenly it seemed impossible that there had ever been any laughter at all. "Only think of it, Brita. I can solve all your problems."

That was not the first time she'd heard that, either, though none of the other men who had said such things to her looked the way Asterion did. His eyes like blue midnight, washed with too many vast, dark seas to count. That stillness that made her whole body want to shake. And shake some more.

As if the sickness was spreading.

"My problems don't need solving. Not by you." She sounded cross and didn't do much to make that stop. "I've already solved them myself."

"Have you?" He did not sound convinced, and for some reason, that was the most disconcerting part of this.

"I have done this a thousand times," she told him. "That is only a slight exaggeration. They propose, I decline. They tell me they can make my life better in this way or that, but what they mean is, they are willing to settle my family's debts and expect me to express my gratitude. When I refuse them yet again, they generally become loud and unpleasant and usually quite red in the face. I really can't take my final vows fast enough."

And she knew that was not the wisest sort of speech to make to a man when he'd just done most of the things she'd listed off. But it was like the night he'd asked her what she wanted to do with her life, and she'd told him and had expected him to demand she apologize the way everyone else did. For all her unseemly *passion*.

Brita only knew that if the man who had just kissed her like that, if that could even be called a *kiss,* got garrulous and flushed, it would sour something inside her. Possibly for good.

But he showed no signs of growing red about his face. And when she spoke, he did not sound anything but…smooth. Dark. *Intense.* "Let me ask you this then, little huntress. How many nuns do you think come alive in a kiss like that?"

And her own heart seemed to work against her, pounding much too hard inside her chest, but she didn't dare reply to that the way she wanted to and launch herself toward him. Even she knew that was a bridge too far. "Perhaps all of them. They have all had their year filled with temptations, perhaps far greater than that."

Though she doubted that very much.

Asterion only watched her, and there was something so knowing in his gaze, so *certain.* It should have made her furious. She should have decried his condescension right then and there.

But that was not, at all, the reaction she had.

Instead, her breath was a shaky thing inside her and she couldn't decide if she wanted to hide it or let him see, because either one seemed equally treacherous just then.

"I need a wife," he said after a while, his midnight eyes gleaming. "And not just any wife, Brita. I need you."

"I have heard that before, too," she informed him, as if her throat wasn't the least bit dry, "and it is never complimentary. Normally it leaves me with the impression that if I were to commission a life-size doll of myself and hand it over in my place, it would serve the same purpose."

She was sure she could feel his laughter inside her again, though she only saw a hint of it in his gaze.

"Many men are collectors," he agreed. "But I am not one of them. The only things I collect are empires, and it has been suggested I already have enough."

"You're very comfortable in your arrogance." That was one way of putting it. Another way was that it made her more *uncomfortable* than it should. "I can say that for you."

His dark eyes gleamed brighter. "Can it be called arrogance when it is nothing less than the simple truth? I do not think so. My grandmother wishes for me to marry, you see. She thinks that it is high time I do something about this reputation of mine. This Monster of the Mediterranean. She is under the impression that a wife will civilize me."

Brita considered that. "I'm afraid that does not sound entirely achievable. No matter who you marry."

"Whether I agree or do not, she has already picked out my bride for me. And I am sorry to tell you that she is the sort of woman who does not permit any deviation from the plans she makes."

Brita also liked a plan, so she nodded at that. But when Asterion only gazed back at her, expectantly, Brita felt that achy heat rush through her all over again.

And this time it was brighter than ever.

"Me?" she managed to ask.

Though there was no reason at all that she should find it difficult to speak.

Asterion only lifted one dark, arrogant brow. "Of course, you."

Another suspicion moved in her, and she let that into her scowl, too, because it felt a bit like armor. And she did not want to think why she needed it, just then, when she had never cared about the things men said. But she did. "There was never any crying creature on your cliff top, was there?"

"That sounds almost poetic." He shrugged, and though it was an arrogant gesture, it was different from before. She was tempted to imagine the great Asterion Teras felt a touch of shame himself. "I'm sure that some poor creature or another has found reason to cry there."

Brita rolled her eyes. "I don't know what makes you think that I would wish to marry an avowed liar."

But the truly strange thing was that she ought to be far more outraged by his games than she was, and she couldn't account for it.

Asterion smiled again, and it was stupid, she thought crossly, that a smile was all he needed to do and she could *feel* it as if he was the one in control of her body, not her. It was an odd new fact she'd discovered tonight and could now file away with the rest. Like the smell of the hills where no one dared walk, right after a rain, like green was a feeling. Like the blue Mediterranean sky above and the sea all around, the color of home.

And now this smile.

He looked at her as if she'd said all of that out loud, and she couldn't be entirely sure she hadn't. "I could wax rhapsodic about each and every one of your attributes, but I suspect you have heard it all before. Tell me, have any of these suitors of yours kissed you?"

She bristled at that. "Certainly not."

"Do you wish they had?"

"Never." She didn't understand why she was flushing then, only that she couldn't seem to stop. "Men are always trying to paw me. That's why I had to learn how to protect myself. The bow and arrow are not my only weapons, you know."

"I should hope not." He reached out, almost languidly. Or more, as if she'd issued him some kind of invitation. As he brushed the backs of his fingers over one hot cheek, then the other, she rather wondered if she had. "You are an adventurer, Brita. You prefer a canopy of stars to any four-poster bed. Your best friend appears to be a besotted wolf." When she looked at him more sharply then, for he was the one who had called Heracles a dog, his eyes only gleamed in that way of his, showing her that private amusement. "There are adventures that I can take you on that I do not think you could have with anyone else."

She considered that. Or maybe what she was considering was that heat beneath her skin and the fact he seemed to know it was there. "I don't know what that means."

"It means that a kiss like that is not ordinary." Again he brushed her cheek, but then his hand moved. This time he slid it over her neck to cup her nape and gently pull her toward him.

It didn't occur to her to do anything but go with it.

She didn't *want* to do anything but that. She thought she would die if she didn't get to see what he was *doing*.

Right now, he was still talking, low and intent. "But a kiss like that, as extraordinary as it is, can only be the beginning. There are worlds to discover, all the many things a man and a woman can teach each other about pleasure. So many horizons to explore. If you dare."

"I'm supposed to enter the convent," she said, but her voice was little more than a faint thread of sound. "Soon."

"Is the convent going somewhere?" Again, all that amusement in his gaze when his face was stern. As if he was honed from this same forge that burned in her. "Surely, if this marriage doesn't suit you, it is always possible for you to return to your solitude and prayers."

She felt suffused with that heat. His hand against her skin was a dark, sinful delight, and she had no doubt that this was the temptation she'd been looking for all along.

That he was.

Because until now, she hadn't really understood

the purpose of this year. Until now, she had thought of it as marking time, nothing more. A nostalgic tour of the island, as free as she'd been when she was a small child when no one took the slightest notice of her.

That had been lovely, in its way.

But this was different. This was Asterion Teras with his hands on her body, and that glowing, growing heat between them like a banked flame that could burst into a wildfire at any moment.

He was the sort of sin that was meant to truly tempt her resolve. She understood that.

Brita could still feel the way he had kissed her. As if his mouth on hers had been a brand. And more than that, as if kissing him had plugged her in to the grandest electrical current of all time, when she had considered herself sufficiently *alive* already.

But it was as if she had been calling gray days *bright* the whole of her life, and only now saw what the world looked like when the sun rose on a blue morning.

And the truth was that while Brita could do without the commentary on her beauty, and all the trouble the fact of her beauty had brought her, she quite loved her body. She loved the things that it could do. The places it took her. She loved how strong she was, how agile. She liked the strength in her arms that let her make her bow sing. And the way her hips moved, as if to a sensual music all their own, when the moon was high.

She had loved all of those things for years now,

yet tonight, with the memory of Asterion's mouth on hers and his fingers against her skin, it was as if she was learning her body for the very first time.

And she wanted *more*.

She wanted that sensation. She wanted that fire.

It had never occurred to her that marrying a man could be so easy. That they could do all these lovely things and bask in them. It had always been presented to her as duty and suffering and putting up with something unpleasant for the sake of others— and what could be less appealing than that?

But this was different.

That kiss made her see all of this in a different way. If she married Asterion, it would delight her family. They would get what they wanted and leave her alone. She wouldn't have to join the convent. It had never been her first choice. It had been the better of the choices offered to her, but that wasn't the same thing.

She felt some regret…but only that she didn't feel *more* regret for a place she'd been quite happy for three whole years.

And best of all, he said that there were worlds to discover, and she thought he meant that.

Brita had never had a fever she didn't bounce back from, the same as before, so why should this one be any different?

And it came with so many other benefits. None of her other suitors had interested her at all, but Asterion did. So much she wasn't sure she'd slept a night through since she'd met him. Marrying him was sure to make all that go away. Even sleeping beneath the stars became familiar over time, no matter how spectacular the shine.

Surely he would, too.

"If I marry you, will there be kissing?" she asked.

Brita didn't entirely understand that indulgent gleam in his gaze then, but it made her feel slick between her legs.

"If you wish."

"Because I've heard my father and stepmother shout at each other about their marriage," she told him, frowning. "And my married cousin is very indiscreet. They all say the same things. They talk of sex a lot, mostly in terms of not having any or using it as currency, but they never kiss." And this time she not only saw that laughter in his gaze, she could feel it in him, as if she was shaking silently with it. "Is that normal?"

"I have never been married, Brita," he told her, as if he was choosing his words very carefully indeed. "But I can promise you that if you marry me, you will have as much kissing as you want and as much sex as I think you can handle."

She didn't like that. "Why do you get to decide?"

And then she watched as Asterion…changed. *Intensified,* rather. She was breathless in an instant, though he didn't move. Yet somehow, she understood that the man she saw before her now was a far realer version of him than any she had seen before. His hand at her nape tightened, though gently.

Gently, it turned out, was like gas on an open flame.

"Because I am a man of vast appetites," he told her. "And when it comes to my pleasure, I am deadly serious. Most women cannot handle me for more than a night. Do you never stop and wonder why it is I'm considered such a monster?"

"I rather thought it was a labyrinth," she said. "And the name of your company. I thought you *wanted* everyone to think of you that way."

"It is because I eat them alive," he said in that dark, intense manner of his, like he was pressing each word into her body. Like it was some kind of dark magic spell.

But it thrilled her.

It filled her up from the inside with a sharp-edged, brilliant glittering she had never felt before. She wanted to die of the joy of it. She wanted to run from him, but only so that she could leap into the air and soar high above the trees, the hills, this sprawling little island that had been her whole world.

Because she could see, now, that the world was so much bigger and more vast. She could see that touching this man would be worlds within worlds within worlds.

He had said so.

Brita had often wished that she could find that holiness the sisters seemed to access so easily. She had hoped it would come in time. She had prayed that it might.

But now she was fiercely glad that it had not.

"I will marry you," she told him, very matter-of-factly. "But you may not wish to marry me."

"I'm not a man who waffles over his decisions, Brita. You should know this about me from the start." His fingers moved, sending another wave of sensation crashing through her. "I have already said that I wish to marry you."

She had to force herself to focus. "That is all very well, and I'm tempted to hold you to that, but you haven't met my family." One of his dark brows rose, and she sighed. "There's my father to contend with, you see. And he will be a drain upon you forever, demanding money and favors and anything else he can imagine. Then there is his wife, who is worse. That's not even getting into the issue of my cousins. It is easiest if you think of them as one entity, but they are relentless. And if left to their own devices, they will bleed you dry." She waited for him to recoil, but he did not. "I think your grandmother must dislike you very much if she sent you to me."

"My grandmother adores me," he replied with all that confidence of his. "My brother would never admit it, but I am her clear favorite."

"I think you've been much deceived." She shook her head. "But if my family doesn't put you off, which is astonishing, I do have my own conditions."

He laughed again, and she decided she loved that sound. This man laughing made her...*glad*. It was as if he was like any one of the creatures she tended to out in these hills. Ferocious from afar, but surprisingly tender up close, though he showed no one else.

It made her feel another kind of warm, everywhere, that he showed her.

"By all means," Asterion said, that laughter making his voice richer. Deeper. "Tell me what conditions you have and I will meet them. Perhaps you have not heard, little huntress. I have the means and the will to get everything it is I want."

"I had no intention of marrying any of the suitors my family presented to me," she said. "And I know that they had no intention of doing anything for me. It was always a transaction they worked out with my father first. But the sisters intended to look into the idea of some kind of refuge. That's what I want."

"My family owns more property on this island than anyone else, save the crown." His tone was so offhand that she wasn't sure she followed him. Again, he raised a brow. "It should be no trouble whatsoever to give some of it over to you. You can do as you wish with it."

"The sisters promised to put it to a robust discussion and give it up in prayer." Brita smiled. "But from you, I think I will require it in writing."

"This is what I like about you." Though, as he growled that out, she was not entirely sure that he did. "You're always surprising."

"Well," she said after a moment, aware that she was too hot again, "I suppose I'm glad that I decided not to let my arrow pierce your flesh. That would have been awkward."

Asterion moved closer. The air all around them got thin. "If you wish for me to kiss you more, Brita, now that we are to be married, all you need do is ask."

But all she could do was nod. Mutely.

And this time it was a slow thing, the way he tugged her toward him. The way he tipped her head back and then settled his mouth to hers.

That was a lesson all on its own, that it could be so different. That it could be the same two people, the same mouths coming together.

That it could be called a kiss but be so *different*.

It was as if every shift of his mouth against hers peeled another layer of her skin away. But not her actual skin. It was like layers of her soul.

Brita moved closer, winding her arms around his neck and pressing herself against him because everything in her body urged her on.

He shifted so that he was holding her there, one hand tangled in her hair and the other a small miracle of sensation and heat up and down the line of her spine.

On and on he kissed her, and it felt like too many things at once. Like soaring high in the sky as she'd imagined, and yet as if there was nothing else but this.

As if the whole of the world narrowed down to his lips, his tongue, his teeth.

As if there was nothing left of her but the way it felt to press her breasts into the hard wall of his chest and try to follow what he did, so he could feel as marvelous as she did, too.

And all the while there was that wild, joyful ache she wanted to go on forever.

For a while it felt as if it did.

But too soon he was pulling back again, and there

was something different about his face, she thought. Something different from before.

"Come," he said, his voice gruff. "There is a wedding to plan. And your grasping, social climbing, currently indebted family to appease. Not to mention, you must present yourself before my grandmother. For an inspection, to be clear. Not just of you. But of us."

"She will want to make certain that this is not a trick." Brita nodded. "I'm all for it. I like her already."

And then her breath left her again when he took her hand, winding his fingers through hers.

Something she had never understood the point of, until now. But his fingers moved slightly as they began to walk, and every bit of friction made that ache in her double. Every bit of friction kept her aware and amazed and shivery from her scalp to the soles of her feet.

It was like that until he let her go, so she could find her way to her night's shelter.

And that was why it was not until the next morning, when she woke up in her campsite, with a grin on her face and an edgy need coursing through her body, that the expression he had on his face after that second kiss came back to her.

It was different from the first time. The first time, he had looked stunned. Almost shaken.

The second time, he had looked indulgent. In control.

She could admit that she found both alluring.

Just remembering them made her breath go shallow.

But there was something in her that told her—with a certainty born of a wisdom deep inside her that she could not name, though she found she trusted it implicitly—that the real man was in that first kiss.

That the control was a defense.

And it was up to her to dismantle it, if she dared.

Smiling up at a bright blue dawn, Brita rather thought she did.

CHAPTER SEVEN

THEIR WEDDING DAY dawned bright and beautiful, as if Asterion had ordered it specifically from the gods to honor his name—or to celebrate the fact that he was achieving the very thing his grandmother had dared suggest he could not do. He was marrying a woman of noted and widely known virtue, despite his reputation.

Despite his well-documented *monstrousness*.

He would have ordered a complimentary rainbow or two from all the gods, old and new alike, had he known how to contact them.

His staff had been working at a frenzied pace ever since he'd announced his engagement, racing to cajole by any means necessary the required officials and priests to move more quickly than usual. And much more quickly than they liked. Asterion was fairly certain that his grandmother's favorite church, the setting she would have preferred for the ceremony, had coldly extorted him to bypass the usual restrictions. The bishop himself had come in to grumble and frown and ultimately do as Asterion wished.

Most did.

Their proper engagement had occurred a week after the night they'd kissed. First he had apprised his staff and sent them off to change the world to suit him. Then he had gone to see the Martis family the very next day.

He had presented himself at the front door of the villa, bright and early. Though he had stood there some while, for it had taken a great deal of knocking and ringing to gain admittance. Then even longer to wait on the family in what must once have been a truly elegant receiving room.

Elegant was not the word for it any longer. The walls were notably cracked. There were indications that paintings had been removed from the walls. The seating arrangements looked as if they had been tossed together, suggesting that whatever elegance had once resided here, it had long since become a bit more of a jumbled collection of odds and ends dragged in from the rest of the sad, old house.

There was no dust. But bitterness seemed to hang over the room just the same, weighing down the beams of sunlight from outside that dared attempt to penetrate it.

This was the very room that boasted the windows he had crept past in the shadows the first night he had met Brita. It was no surprise that it was not a pleasant place.

He had been equally unsurprised at the hollow-eyed, clearly hungover family members who trickled in to greet him—eventually—because their appearances matched the harsh voices he'd heard that night.

There were roughly seven of them in total, assuming no more were lurking about in the villa, unable to rise to the occasion. The man, who he took to be Vasilis Martis. The clearly vain and overly precious woman at his side, who'd made it clear she was his wife. He saw a woman of about Brita's age, who could only be the cousin she had mentioned, looking haughty and unfriendly. And two other males of the same features, marking them as members of the same clan, one with a sour-faced woman who sat beside him with ill grace.

Asterion disliked them all on sight.

"I cannot say we are normally descended upon at such an uncivil hour," the stepmother said in a querulous voice.

"Forgive me the intrusion," Asterion had said in return, in a tone that made it clear he expected that forgiveness to be a foregone conclusion. "But I come to you with joyful news." He trained his gaze on Brita's father. "Your daughter, sir, has consented to make me the happiest man alive. So it is that I, Asterion Teras, will be taking Brita as my wife, and in so doing, joining your family to mine." He'd inclined his head. "I offer you my felicitations."

Brita had told him exactly what to expect, and he had quickly discovered that she had been right on every score. Down to the surly expressions on each of her relatives' faces at such an early hour. At first they had thought that she might join in this particular scene, but had decided that it would go just as well without her.

Because it wasn't really about her, was it?

And sure enough, the family only looked at each other in astonishment for a few short moments. Then their surprise was quickly overtaken by a far more powerful force.

Greed.

"My daughter is an heiress to the family name and entirely too dear to us," her father had demurred, his gaze alight with dreams of wealth. "I cannot possibly allow *just anyone* to walk in off the street and marry her. Surely you must know that she is in great demand."

"The difference being that she wishes to marry me," Asterion had pointed out silkily.

And it was a mark of how well they all knew precisely who he was, and how little they were inclined to doubt a man with his portfolio, that no one questioned that. Even though Brita had thus far shown no interest in marrying anyone else that had been paraded before her.

There were certainly no calls to bring Brita forth, that she might assure them of the truth of Asterion's claim.

I can assure you, all they need to know about you is that you are...you, Brita had assured him, laughing, though Asterion had found it...significantly less amusing.

And he found it even less so as he witnessed them all behaving precisely as she had predicted.

Her father had leaned forward in his chair, his smile thin, though his eyes still danced. No doubt doing sums in his head and planning his spending. "There are certain considerations," he began.

But Asterion was not an empire builder by accident, even if he was more unsettled by this clinical exchange than he wished to let on. He told himself that it was a good reminder that this marriage would be a contract like any other, and he would control its outcome as he did anything else he chose to sign his name to.

Still, that odd sensation persisted. He was…disconcerted.

Not that he let it show. He leaned back against the nearest mantel, propped himself up as if he was bored, and inclined his head.

"Go on then," he'd said. "Name your price."

And the bargaining had begun in earnest.

Only when that unsavory task was done and the contracts all signed had he brought Brita to see his grandmother.

He had considered putting her in the sort of formal attire that he knew his grandmother preferred, but he didn't. Dimitra was the one who had chosen Brita, and so she could meet the real Brita, in all her glory.

There was ample time to dress her for the role she would need to take on—at least in public—to bring the expected glory to the Teras name.

"Why did you pick me to marry him?" Brita had asked, the moment she and Dimitra had clapped eyes on each other. She hadn't even waited to take a seat on one of the excessively theatrical couches. "I can't imagine why I would be anybody's first choice, and especially not yours."

"You are the only choice," Dimitri had responded, with a cackle. "I rather thought you'd have the good sense to refuse him."

"Well," Brita had murmured, "there's still time."

Asterion supposed that he should not have been surprised that his grandmother found his little huntress delightful. Even though she was nothing like all the heiresses Dimitra had thrown his way in the past, Brita reminded Dimitra of herself. She said so—more than once—and there was no higher compliment his grandmother could bestow.

Once those key meetings were finished, he could get on with the actual engagement.

I suggest you lock that down, his grandmother had told him. *Before she comes to her senses.*

Asterion did not explain to Dimitra that he had a secret weapon. Brita would do almost anything he asked if it would lead to more kissing, and he knew it.

He no longer had any doubt about his ability to control the situation because he controlled the pace. She was an innocent and he was not, and there was no need to worry about *losing himself.* That had been a momentary bit of madness out there in the moonlight—but once they were married, he would not have to worry about such things. They would settle. They would no longer be so *fraught.*

The unsettled sensation would be a memory, nothing more.

Still, he did not tarry. He had talked to Brita about the worlds he would show her, for all of them were at his feet. She had seemed duly unimpressed. And when he asked her where she might like to go, she had named Paris as the city she would most like to see.

She had first named a number of inaccessible wildernesses, to be fair. There were mountains she wanted to climb. Seas she wished to swim. Impossible glaciers she wished to stand upon, for no good reason that he could discern. Yet something about the shiny newness of her enthusiasm got to him. It made him want nothing more than to show her all the things she could imagine, and many more, and explore them all with her and that clear-eyed wonder she brought with her wherever she went.

Another man might have imagined himself besotted.

Asterion, happily, was not another man.

When it came to their engagement, a man of his status had certain expectations attached to him. There were tried-and-true ways that he needed to make certain announcements to the world at large, and a city was needed.

Once again, Brita surprised him. Not only with the choice of Paris, a city many loved the world over but he had not expected she would care for one way or the other, but because she bargained with him there, too.

There were a whole host of museums she wanted to see and cultural monuments she wanted to visit, and only then would she condescend to visit the atelier he had selected to handle the details of her wardrobe.

"I can dress myself," she told him on the flight over, frowning at him over the breakfast the staff had prepared and served them in the cabin of his private plane.

"I do not see the purpose of having a wife if I cannot dress her to my taste," he had replied offhandedly.

She had eyed him. "Like a blow-up doll, you mean."

"Like the man who intends to remove every article of clothing I pay to put on you," he had replied. Just quietly enough.

And had enjoyed very much the shade of pink she took on for the rest of the flight.

That night, he took her out to dinner at a restaurant that did not take reservations and rarely had seatings—unless a person possessed the sort of name that did not require such pedestrian concerns. Asterion was, naturally, one of them. And it was a deeply pleasurable thing indeed to watch Brita experience new flavors, new culinary artistry, new sensual delights.

Halfway through the meal, he found himself thinking that he would need to make it a priority to introduce her to as many new things as possible, just to watch her immerse herself in these experiences. To be the one sitting with her when she raised her gaze, wide with awe, when something charmed or surprised her.

The way he wanted her would have concerned him, he was sure, if he was someone else. If he had to worry about being unable to control himself.

He had to remind himself that he was Asterion Teras, and he was above such things, no matter what he might find himself feeling in a Parisian restaurant in the company of a woman who only he knew was a wild virgin huntress, like all the myths of old, capable of shooting bows and befuddling men with a single glance.

Afterward, he walked her out into the fireworks display that was the paparazzi waiting for them outside with a ring on her finger that he had put there during the meal. It was a masterwork of a diamond. It was flawless and breathtakingly elegant, yet somehow called to mind the sweet clarity of her hilltops, the moon that had risen before them, and the way she had kissed him, all fire and fury.

"It seems a bit much," Brita had said inside, turning it this way and that.

"I am a bit much, little huntress," he had replied. "And more."

But he had breathed easier than he wanted to admit when she looked at him and smiled.

Rumors of their engagement—or, rather, Asterion Teras's engagement to a mysterious woman in fashionable Paris—made it into the papers before the plane touched down on the island later that same night.

It had been chaotic ever since, and made both worse and better because there were far fewer midnight rambles on the hillsides. Asterion had to be quite stern with himself. Once they were married, he could not allow such security risks. To say nothing of the time commitment. There would have to be no more of such foolishness.

Once they were married, he assured himself, they would have other ways of entertaining themselves.

And now, at last, the wedding day had come. His brother had made an appearance, down from London, which he claimed he preferred to the island. The priests had been appeased and an altar had been set up on Asterion's property, which was ever after to remain a holy place. He had agreed easily enough, for he already considered it holy enough. It was his.

Dimitra had insisted on taking part in the expansive guest list, and so, between her connections and his contacts, it was the breathtakingly sophisticated affair a Teras wedding should be, staged out on the cliffs above his home.

Even Brita's family seemed disposed to behave themselves, no doubt because the wedding itself was the grandest affair any of them had attended in generations.

Dimitra, true to her word as ever, elected to pretend she did not see them.

And finally Asterion stood at the head of the aisle that led to his new chapel, arranged to make sure that anyone watching could not fail to take in the view of the sea that seemed to stretch on into eternity. He could see that more than one guest was duly enchanted.

But he rather liked the vision coming toward him.

Brita on her father's arm in a flowing white dress that was remarkable in its simplicity.

On another woman, it might have been drab. Too plain. She had spent some while discussing the matter at the atelier in Paris and had decided that less was more.

For she was already too beautiful for her own good. Too beautiful for his peace of mind. She did not need adornments and so the dress had none.

She left her hair down and wore a sort of crown of flowers, as if to remind everyone that she was only as civilized as she pretended to be, and only for the moment. Asterion took the message to heart.

But what mattered more was that her eyes were on him.

And then her hands were in his.

Once that happened, he no longer cared about anything else. Only the promise in her eyes and the sound of her voice repeating their simple, ancient vows.

And when he kissed her, making her his wife at last, he felt as if she almost undid him that easily.

When he could not allow himself to be undone.

"We are married," she said solemnly as they walked back down the aisle together.

"Well and truly," he agreed.

And he could not have said why that felt like a storm inside him, rising into full roar.

But the reception was a grand party, and a reprieve. There were people to talk to, a meal to eat, and all the usual speeches, and he told himself he was glad of it all even if he didn't care about any of it.

All he could think about was what would come later.

When he could stand it no longer, he stole Brita away from the people already cozying up to her, the new Teras wife, which might have been amusing if he wasn't so riddled with his need for her. He drew her out onto the dance floor they'd made in his gardens, because it was the next best thing to what he really wanted.

When there were still hours to go.

She swayed with him, lithe and too lovely, tipping her head back so she could study his face.

For once in his life, he had no idea what might be found there.

"How much longer do we have to do all this?" she asked.

And it was easier then. She'd broken the worst of the tension in him and so he could smile.

Better yet, he could pretend that she was the impatient one. "How shocking of you, Brita," he murmured. "All of these people have assembled to celebrate our joy."

"They have assembled to dance attendance on one of the wealthiest men in the world," she replied in her matter-of-fact way that, after so many conversations tonight that were circuitous and treacherous, struck him like a deep breath of good air. "And the strange wild woman he's chosen for a wife."

"Surely you must know that they are attempting to curry your favor as well."

"I cannot be curried," she assured him. Then smiled. "But I do enjoy the attempts. They do not realize that I can only think of one thing."

"Are you so single-minded?" he asked, not quite lazily, though he did not think he should let her know how her words hit at him.

"You know what I want," she told him.

He had signed the documents she'd requested with great flourish, though he made a point to inform her that no one else had ever dared question his word. That his promise to make her the wildlife refuge she wanted should have sufficed.

But he knew that for once, island wildlife was not what was heaviest on her mind.

Not tonight.

"Don't you worry," he told her as they danced, swaying together like a premonition. A glimpse into the future that made him perilously close to embarrassing himself. "I will have my mouth all over you, little huntress. I will make you scream."

And when she kissed him as the song ended, he could feel the hint of her teeth.

"You have your hands full there," Poseidon said idly when Asterion found his brother at the bar, enjoying the attentions of a full rugby scrum of beautiful women. All of whom scattered before Asterion and his monstrous reputation.

He'd had the idle thought that perhaps his marriage would change that, but apparently it hadn't yet.

"I think I'll be just fine," Asterion replied to his brother, smiling in what he could only describe as full elder brother.

"Is it true what they say? She roams the hills, bow and arrow in hand, as one with the wild things?"

Asterion smiled. "Not tonight."

The reception carried on, glittering on into the night, until Asterion began to wonder if it would last forever—trapping him in this strange space where he could never quite touch Brita the way he wished he could.

The way, he could admit now, he had imagined he would too many times to count.

It was becoming too much like that sickness Brita had mentioned. He had never felt its like.

Then again, he had also never denied himself something he wanted for this long.

"And you thought I couldn't do this," he chided his grandmother as he danced with her, something that might have been sentimental in another family.

But they were the last of the Teras dynasty and their dance with so many eyes upon them was a demonstration of power. Marking their legacy and their intention to continue it, just as Dimitra wanted.

"Have you wooed her?" Dimitra asked with too much wisdom in her voice for his liking. As if she was being prophetic. He knew she was only being herself, which was to say, nosy.

"I have wed her," Asterion retorted. "So what does wooing matter, in the end?"

"You," his grandmother said, turning her gleaming gaze on him as they moved across the dance floor, "are a very foolish man."

And Asterion would normally take exception to a statement like that, but he couldn't. Not tonight.

Because *foolish* was the only word to describe how his brand-new wife made him feel, and he did not intend to admit that to anyone.

He could barely admit it to himself.

And just when he was beginning to believe that they were to be stuck in the endless purgatory of this wedding forever, the reception was finally over. His staff ushered the guests out of the gardens, guiding them along with bright lanterns while Asterion and Brita stood before the grand dome that served as the entrance to his labyrinth and waved them off.

Until, at last, they were gone.

His staff melted back around to the cliff side of the house to handle the cleanup, and after all this time, he was alone with his wife.

No staff. No crowd. No one but them.

It felt almost too good to be true.

Asterion hadn't meant to move, but somehow they were facing each other once more, standing there as if they were about to take their vows all over again.

And he could feel his pulse overtaking him, that fire in his blood crowding out his ability to do anything but breathe.

But barely.

The breeze tainted him with that scent of hers that he knew matched her taste—a little bit herbal, a touch of green. And then the sweetness that was only her.

He thought he ought to say something, for he was the one with experience here. Though at the moment he couldn't recall any of it. Instead, he felt like the callow, overset boy he had never been.

The stars seemed to press in. The dark seemed too thick, suddenly, and far hotter than it should have been this time of year.

And Brita, who should have been the one trembling and beside herself, overcome at what might happen now, smiled.

She took a step back, gave him a speaking sort of glance as she turned, and then melted off toward the trees.

Right before she disappeared into the trees, she looked back over her shoulder and raised her brows in a clear and obvious challenge.

And he was lost.

Asterion was after her without another thought, like the wild animal he prided himself on never allowing himself to become—

Except for tonight.

CHAPTER EIGHT

BRITA WAITED FOR HIM, this brand-new husband of hers, when she had never imagined she would marry unless under the deepest duress, in the soft embrace of the trees.

He was there in a flash, his chest heaving as if he'd run the whole way, when she knew very well he hadn't. She had watched him walk toward her, filled with purpose. She had caught her breath as she waited, and now that he was close, she could see his eyes were dark with the same passion she felt storming inside her.

It was a marvel, that she should like everything about this night.

And about this man.

She liked that her body seemed caught between thunder and lightning, both hitting her at once. She liked how his gaze caught her as surely as any well-aimed arrow, so she felt trapped in the most delicious way possible.

It didn't occur to her to attempt to move.

She would have fought against it if anyone else dared try and move her.

And these were funny thoughts indeed for a woman who had, until so recently, imagined that the only future worth having involved holy orders.

"Husband," she said, testing the word in her mouth. "You're my *husband*."

"And you, little huntress, are my wife," he replied in that same dark, thrilling manner.

She had been there at their wedding. It had been remarkably elegant. She'd spent the better part of it convinced that at any moment, she would shame herself by dumping her food down the front of her white gown, tripping over the hem of it, or otherwise making it clear that she was unequal to the task of becoming a Teras wife.

That was what the papers said. She'd hated it— all those cameras, the endless flashes as if she was caught in a storm again but this time, the lightning hit. And hit. And hit again.

But the true blows had come later, when the papers had opined about her worthiness to marry the scion of the Teras family. They paraded her family's history before the world, and while Brita could not disagree with the conclusions drawn about her father, his wife, and her cousins, she also found she did not care for it when others spoke ill of them.

They called her insulting names. *Like gold digger.*

She wanted to correct them. She wanted to tell the world that actually she alone cared nothing for the man's money and wanted him only for his much-vaunted sexual prowess—but in order to do that, she would have to confess to Asterion that the things the papers said bothered her.

And she couldn't.

She wouldn't.

It had been impressed on her a long, long time ago that it was always better to be the one who cared less. And that the less she appeared to care, the more she got what she wanted. Like university.

And this time what she wanted was so huge it terrified her.

She would act unbothered—by everything—if it killed her, because the alternative was unthinkable.

Brita was well aware that most of the guests already thought that she was exactly as unworthy of Asterion as the papers had speculated, at great length. Some hadn't even bothered to conceal their sneers.

She had concentrated on the part of her that was tempted to trip *and* stain herself anyway, knowing that whatever shame she felt personally, if she revealed herself to be so embarrassing at such a moment her father would likely leap straight off the side of the cliff before them.

It really had been tempting.

But a wedding was a play that everyone already knew the words to, so that made it both easier and stranger. Brita had been aware of all those eyes on her, but she was used to being stared at. The people in the villages had always made it clear that she was different in ways they didn't quite like, though they had never taken to it with the nasty glee of the gutter press. But the looks from Asterion's posh friends and associates had been far more…assessing. Maybe even intrigued.

And then there'd been the clasping of hands as she'd gazed into Asterion's eyes and the ancient vows they'd recited word for word. The wedding crowns. The three trips around the altar while every member of her family glared at her from the front row.

No doubt they'd been concerned that at any moment Heracles might put in an appearance, or worse, Brita might shame herself—meaning, them—but it had all gone smoothly. Then there had been dinner. Dancing. Endless discussions with people whose names she had no interest in remembering. There had been all the jostling for position and suggestions of influence that she had discussed with Asterion earlier, all of which bored her, but none of that mattered now.

All of that had been for others. The pageantry. The customs. The endless celebrating that had all been for specific reasons, none of them Asterion and her.

But now it was only the two of them, out here in the dark.

Now, at last, they were down to the only things that mattered.

The two of them out in the night with nobody watching, the way it had been at the start or none of this would have happened.

And so it made all the sense in the world that it was here he reached out, drew her to him, and kissed her—

But this time in a way she knew, somehow, he did not mean to stop anytime soon.

It all seemed to hit her the way it always did when he was near. That great flush, that ache, and all the ways she *wanted something* she couldn't define.

It was easy to call it *itchy,* but it felt like something more.

Because as she pressed herself against the wide wall of his chest, she felt both more and less of all those things. As if he was the cure as well as the disease.

But Brita didn't care what he was. She wound herself around him, jumping up so she could wrap her legs around his waist. Then she sighed a little as he gripped her by the thighs and held her there.

And still he kissed her, on and on, all of it fire.

All of it starshine and moonlight, tangling around inside of her so that all she could do was hold on to him with every part of her that she could think to use, and then see where the storm would take her.

Then, maybe, she would find out what was left of her—if anything—when it blew itself out.

And when he laid her out on the ground, the soft bed she liked best, Brita could hardly tell the difference between the tumble inside her and how it felt to be tipped flat on her back and pressed down.

But she knew she liked that, too.

His hands cupped her face and he kissed her again, deep and wild. Then he tore his mouth from hers and set it to her cheek, her temple, teaching her new ways to burn.

Until she wondered if he meant to turn every last part of her to ash.

And if she would laugh happily into the night while she turned to flame, the way she did now as he went lower still, finding the pulse in her neck, her collarbone.

Then it was as if a great, shattering earthquake overtook them both, because she could feel a trembling within her and in him, too, in every place their bodies touched. In every place he pressed all his strength and heat against her.

In all the places she was soft.

He made a noise that made her think of the wildest things, too wild to let her near, and she felt it echo deep within her.

Something in her whispered, *yes*.

So she indulged herself and let her hands move all over him, finding the astonishing shape of him beneath his clothes, then shoving her fingers through any odd buttonhole she could to find the heat of him and the hard, smooth muscles that made his chest more like a feast than the dinner they'd sat through earlier.

And the more she touched him, the more everything seemed better.

Wilder, yes. Hotter, *yes, please*.

"We must go slow," he warned her, right when she thought she might sink her teeth into him just to see how he would taste. "For you are new and untried, and I fear—"

"I fear nothing," she told him, though she pulled back.

Then paused, her heart a new thunder in her chest, because he looked something like tortured.

But after a considering breath, Brita decided that only made her feel bolder.

She reached down and grabbed the hem of her dress and began to pull it up, baring herself to him.

And was glad she did, because he made another one of those noises, like a wild thing.

Brita didn't need to ask if that was approval. She knew it was.

It was as if she suddenly understood the purpose of her body in a whole new way. She had long expected it to be able to run. To hike and climb. To dance in the rain and bathe in the moonlight.

But this was something brand-new.

There was that scalding heat between her legs. It made her want to shiver. Maybe she did. And still, all she wanted to do was press herself to him, twine herself around him, and see how much hotter she could get.

When she did, she could feel that thick, hot ridge between his legs, and that made everything inside her seem to *shimmer*.

"Little huntress, you don't understand—" he began.

But she didn't want to understand.

She wanted to follow these sensations, and so she reached out her hand and put it to the front of his trousers. Then she felt for the shape of him, finding herself grinning, then laughing, at the rich, deep sounds he made.

He growled, like any other wild beast, and it was a thrilling sound.

It seemed to fill her up—and then Asterion had her flat on her back.

She didn't even feel him move.

One moment she was laughing, then he loomed over her, on top of her, propping himself up on one elbow as he reached between them. And she did not have to know precisely what he was doing to know exactly what he was doing. Every hair on her body seemed to prickle into awareness.

It was possible she made her own sort of growling noise and got a flash of that midnight blue for her troubles.

But then he focused his attention on the important work of opening his wedding trousers, then taking that great shaft of his and working it all over and through that wetness between her legs.

"You do not wear underthings," he gritted out, as if the knowledge hurt him.

"They seem extraneous," she replied.

And then she forgot about it, because he was *moving*.

It was like magic.

It was extraordinary.

She'd never felt another person's hands on her, much less on her intimate parts, and certainly not *there*.

Asterion dragged himself through all that heat, once, then again, and then suddenly, something seemed to buckle up from within her. She tried to dance in it, like any storm, but she couldn't—

Because before she could find her footing, she

was shimmering and burning bright, tumbling out into the universe.

When she was herself again, Asterion was still there, holding himself above her.

She felt the flame start within her all over again.

His eyes were glittering with the dark madness she felt everywhere, and then she watched as he pressed that same part of him into the core of her need.

Everything shook, but she didn't quite *shimmer*—

And then, his eyes on hers, he pushed himself inside her, but only a little.

Then he pulled out again, and the next time, he went a little further—a new need, a new lightning, shooting out from everywhere he touched her, centering deep inside and then fanning out, to light up every last part of her body.

Every limb. Every bone.

Everything she was or ever would be.

And on and on he worked himself inside her, inch by beautiful, treacherous, glorious inch.

Until, at last, he was firmly seated deep within her body.

She heard a high-pitched, strange new sound.

"Breathe," Asterion told her in that dark way of his that she found not even remotely grim, not now.

When she pulled in that breath he'd commanded, she realized that she was the one making that noise. That she was panting wildly, or maybe she was moaning—she didn't know.

But when she bore down on that great, hot length

of him inside her, filling her up, pressing her from the inside out, surely too big and too thick to fit—

She broke apart once again,

This time, as she came back down, she heard the sound of his laughter—that dark, not quite musical threat that made everything in her hum with fresh delight.

And then he began to move.

This was not the easing in, then out, from before.

This was different. This was so very different—

But Asterion was in control. He set them a rhythm and did not stray from it.

And all Brita could think to do was hold on to him as best she could, her grip tight and her head thrown back to take in all of it, as he taught her things she never could have guessed about her own body.

About pleasure and desire.

About the kind of passion she had never believed was real.

Again and again, he thrust deep and made her new.

Until finally, she flew apart a third time and he flew with her, catapulting them both out to all the galaxies that spun high above until she couldn't tell the difference between them and her.

Maybe they were all the same.

It was possible she simply disappeared, for a time.

Because she had no memory of him moving away from her, dressing them both in some fashion or another, then swinging her up into his arms. But these things must have happened, because when she knew herself again he was striding back toward that house of his, toward that gleaming globe that rose from the earth, holding her in his arms as if she was some kind of sacrifice.

And Brita had never particularly wished to sacrifice herself for anything, but tonight, she found she did not mind.

She let her head rest on his shoulder and she stared out at the sea as he took her down and then down farther into his labyrinth, down one set of stairs and then another, all of them encased in glass, until he took her into what she assumed must be his bedroom.

He set her on the edge of a very wide, very high bed and then, his eyes glittering once again, he set about stripping her entirely of everything she wore once more—save the crown of flowers on her head that was only slightly askew.

"You look like a goddess," he told her, his voice rough.

Brita liked that. Every part of her body felt alive and new. The tips of her breasts stood up proudly, begging for his attention. Between her legs, she was softer and hotter than before. That itchiness, that ache—she understood what it was now and she welcomed those sensations as they made her skin feel too tight and yet just right.

And when he knelt down the side of the bed and spread her legs wide before him, she found herself holding her breath.

Then letting it out in a rush as he pulled her thighs

over his shoulders, leaned in, and licked his way into her softness.

Where he taught her a whole new way to move, to dance, to rock herself against the wild seduction of his mouth.

When she was sobbing and falling apart, he stood. She could only half watch him, too busy trying to breathe, as he stripped himself of what was left of his own clothes, presenting himself marvelously naked before her at last.

Brita wanted so many things then.

And all of them at once.

That terror of it was almost too much.

She wanted to bury her face between the slabs of muscle that made up his chest. She wanted to follow that trail of hair down to where it ended at that great shaft of his. She wanted to taste him as he tasted her.

But she did none of those things because what he did was crawl over her, then roll so that she was sitting on top of him, her hair falling between them like a dark, silken curtain that smelled of the things his staff had put in it instead of earth and fire, fresh air and growing things.

Brita did not dislike the scent as much as she thought she should.

And then she stopped caring, because his hands were on her hips, shifting her, and she could feel him pressed into her again.

But this time from a completely different angle.

"Surely you know how to ride," he said, more than a little challenge in his voice.

Brita accepted the challenge. She propped herself up against his chest, pressing the heel of her palms against him, already trembling because it was her turn to move.

And oh, how she wanted to.

So she did.

She lifted herself, then sank down, groaning at the differences in the way he filled her. She writhed against him, following all those longings inside her. She leaned forward and found it was even better when he found her nipple with his mouth and wilder sensations streaked through her like a new way to burn.

She didn't think she could match his rhythm, so she indulged herself instead, making them both dance to a beat of her own making and not stopping no matter how intense it became.

No matter how hard he gripped her hips.

And soon enough, she was catapulting straight for another explosion—

And Asterion took control, hammering into her, making it clear that he knew exactly what every stroke was doing to her—

Until together they ignited, burned like a comet, and then dropped back down into this bed of his.

And the dark of the room swallowed them whole, until, tangled up together, she slept.

At some point he woke her and there were wet cloths and low murmurs she hardly understood.

Still she slept, and when she woke, there were faint notes of peach and orange over the gleaming sea on the far side of the glass, the morning sky a silent symphony stretched out before her. One of her favorite views.

She looked beside her in the wide bed, but Asterion wasn't there.

Brita could admit that there was a part of her that was relieved.

Because she was certain that all of last night was stamped on the skin of her face, or perhaps it had changed the very bone structure she'd had her whole life. She could *feel* it.

All she knew was that she was not the same person she'd been when she'd woken up yesterday.

She was just as glad there was no one else around to see it.

The crown of flowers from the wedding was on the floor beside the bed, and she had no memory of removing it. She was naked, and it was true that she had grown so accustomed to camping, but she did not think that was the only reason that the sheets against her skin felt like a caress.

Nothing in the whole of her life could possibly have prepared her for feeling like this.

For feeling so close, physically and otherwise, to another person.

He had been *inside* her.

His mouth had found parts of her that Brita had never seen with her own eyes. Even now, alone and hours later, she felt shivery all over again—and emotional.

And terrified all over again, and this time worse than before.

Because she had been as innocent as he'd claimed and she'd had no idea that anyone could feel like this.

Vulnerable. Stripped raw. Both wanting more and wanting to run.

As if the emotion inside her was a true fever this time and might burn her alive.

She curled up where she lay, closed her eyes, both shocked and yet unsurprised when moisture leaked from her lashes. And she remembered, almost against her will, the trip she taken to the convent only ten days ago.

Your year is not yet up, child, the Abbess had said when Brita had been brought through to her presence. Though there had been a wise look on her face, as if she already knew what Brita had come to tell her.

I am marrying, Brita had said in her typically blunt way. *But not for the reasons that other people marry. And one day, I think it's entirely possible that I will be back here, hoping to join you once more.*

The Abbess had inclined her head, but when she looked up, she'd only smiled.

Knowingly.

That was all, when Brita had expected a quiet lecture or talk of her duties. Failing that, perhaps a bit of condemnation for straying from the path.

Anything but that smile.

The entire exchange had confused her.

But here in this marriage bed, turned inside out

by the man she had married and already desperate for more, she understood.

Too well, she understood.

Everything had changed.

She had changed, inside and out.

He had changed her.

And she could never go back to the girl she had been before last night.

CHAPTER NINE

A MONTH INTO his new marriage, Asterion had to accept that, despite his intentions, which were usually as good as written law where most things were concerned, it was not going to plan.

The evidence had been all around him, but the final straw was an exquisitely exclusive gala event in Monaco.

Brita, as ever, stunned without trying. She wore the simplest of gowns with little to no adornment because none was needed. She was breathtaking as she walked in, catching every eye without seeming to notice that anyone was looking, which Asterion knew could only add to her mystique. The gossipy papers were filled with speculation about the new Teras wife, but he did not have to counsel Brita on how to ignore the tales they spun—she never paid the slightest attention to such things. She treated rumors and gossip and the usual social machinations by the usual people the same way she did everything else. She sailed on by, smiled enigmatically, and then did precisely as she pleased.

Only he knew that she had spent the drive from

one of his properties, a villa filled with priceless art and Côte d'Azur sunshine on the water in Cap Ferrat, experimenting with different ways to take him in her mouth.

Yet an hour or so into the event she was nowhere to be found.

This was not unusual, and that was the trouble. Other wives stayed with their husbands, particularly when their husbands were rich and powerful tycoons who did as they pleased in their corporate playgrounds. Staying at or near their husbands' sides was part of their expected marital duties. No point having a trophy, after all, if it couldn't be displayed.

He was certain he had expressed this notion to his errant new wife after the last event, where an acquaintance had slyly pretended not to know that Asterion had married, since there was no blushing bride in evidence. And Asterion hoped the man in question had enjoyed himself, because he'd lost himself and his company a lucrative deal thanks to that tone.

Something he had attempted to impress upon his wife.

But he had looked around some fifteen minutes ago tonight and realized that Brita was nowhere to be found. It wasn't that he worried about her or what she might be getting up to—and not because she was of as little interest to him as other women had been.

Quite the opposite.

Some men might be concerned that a wife so beautiful might be off sharing her charms with others, but Asterion had no doubts on that score. Not a one.

Others might worry that the unscrupulous might attempt to use Brita to get to him in one way or another, but he wasn't worried about that, either.

He did not permit her to carry her bow and arrows into polite society, but he had no doubt that if she wished, his wife could defend herself handily. But there was far too much security in a place like this for that to be a factor.

Asterion exhausted the possibilities in the grand ballroom, found no sign of her, and then asked himself where the least likely place would be for a guest to go. He followed the catering staff in through a set of swinging doors, wound his way through the bowels of the fancy old Château, high on a hillside, and found himself in the kitchens.

Then, following an inkling he did not care to acknowledge closely, he let himself out the back door, walked out into the gardens, and found his wife kneeling there on the ground near a bit of shrubbery.

She looked up at him, but showed no hint of shame or apology.

If anything, she was glowing, there in the dirt.

"I found kittens," she told him, with wonder and joy, as if kittens were a scarce resource in this world. "I think they lost their mama."

"Brita," he began, in tones of admonishment.

Then stopped, because she was paying no attention to him.

To *him*.

Instead, as he watched in astonishment, she gathered up seven tiny, mewling little creatures in the skirt of her gown as if it was no more to her than a rag. She paid no attention to the leaves and dirt clinging to her as she marched all the little kittens inside. She found homes for five of them before clearing the kitchen, and then presented the last two to the host himself, out there in the middle of the exquisitely grand Château.

She was a menace.

It occurred to him that she was also, perhaps, doing what she needed to do to find her own way through the pit of vipers and snakes that was the social circle he moved in. He was sympathetic. He was.

But there was the Teras legacy to uphold.

"You do realize the purpose of attending an event is to actually attend it, do you not?" he asked her as they flew back south toward home, much later that night.

She only looked at him dreamily, no doubt with kittens dancing in her head. "Did you give them an obscene amount of money?" When he only lifted a brow, she laughed. "And why not save a few other lives while you're at it? What is the harm?"

The trouble was, the fact that he could not contain her made him...uneasy. Even if this was just how she'd decided to cope with the demands of her new role.

As the month wore on, it only got worse. He never knew what she would do, and he was sure he did not care for it.

At a wedding of minor, yet well-connected, royals in Europe, she befriended the groom's blind old uncle and made a friend of the watchful royal seeing eye dog, winning her the admiration of two kingdoms without even trying.

"What a coup," his number two man crowed. "We have been trying to get past the insistence both countries have on dealing only with local entities for years. One pat of a dog's head and the doors are now open. She's a secret weapon, sir!"

But Asterion knew better.

She was a loaded weapon, and he was not the one aiming it.

Would he use her to advance his business concerns if he could? He told himself he would, even though that, too, made him uneasy for even more reasons he did not care to excavate. Yet he would never know, because he couldn't *tell* Brita to do the things she did. She simply did them, and *she* didn't care how anyone else responded to those things.

Including him, it seemed.

For at home, no matter how many times he told her it was not appropriate for the wife of Asterion Teras to roam about the hills the way she liked to do, and no matter how many times she nodded sagely as if she agreed, she disappeared into the trees whenever she liked. Not as if she hadn't heard him, but as if he had not spoken on the topic at all.

He found he did not know what to do with the part of him that wanted to ask her if her need to always run for the literal hills was an emotional response to him, to their marriage, to the world he'd thrust her into. Because asking her such a question risked the possibility that she might ask him something similar in return.

And he refused to have *emotions*.

No matter what he felt.

Asterion could not decide what was worse. That for the first time, someone else lived in this house he had built for himself alone and he was aware of her presence, always.

Or the fact that when she was gone, he could feel that, too.

And not like a kind of peace.

He was on edge. He was certain that it was affecting his work—

Though his staff assured him that it was not. By reminding him that he could take the next seventy years off and still increase his annual profits by rote.

It was in this way that Asterion began to find himself behaving like a person he hardly knew.

He waited for her. He *waited up* for her. Sometimes he even roamed about the woods himself, though he never found her.

Making him suspect that she did not wish to be found.

Like she really was a creature made of myth and village lore.

He found himself wondering if it might have been easier if she really had been sneaking out to meet some kind of lover, however little he could imagine a man who could compete with him—and, for once, that was not his arrogance talking.

It was that he knew full well that what happened

between them in bed was as shattering for her as it was for him.

Not that he cared to admit, even to himself, *how* intense it was with Brita. How raw. How different from all the shallow games with sex he realized only now he'd been playing his whole life.

He was not at all certain he liked that he no longer wished to play such games—especially because she clearly did.

And he did not ask himself why it was easier to believe she was playing games than to allow for the possibility that there was more to her behavior than simple caprice.

She would melt in and out of his house, always more silently than should have been possible. He would wait for her in the darkened bedroom and turn on the light when she entered like a ghost. He was always expecting her to flinch, offer stammering apologies, look *even remotely* guilty, but she never did.

"I found a nest of blackcaps," she would tell him, chattily, seeming perfectly happy to see him. Seeming not to notice that he was lurking about in the shadows of his own house like the sort of man he had vowed he would never become. The sort of man he had watched behave too much like this when he was a child, and it was not a comparison he cared for. He did not wish to become his father, a victim to every stray passion. He prided himself on having excised such things from his being, deliberately, since the age of twelve. "I had to make sure they were safe from the foxes."

There was always a reason. It was usually an animal in need, or the opportunity to observe another. Sometimes it was the moon over the water again, or the particular beauty of the stars. And no matter how he attempted to make his displeasure clear, she ignored it.

Brita not only ignored it, she would strip out of the clothes she liked to wear to wander the hills in defiance of his wishes. Then she would put out her hands and walk to him, quickly making him forget why he was outraged with her in the first place.

It took him a whole lot longer than it should have to realize that the way she treated him was eerily familiar, and not because it reminded him of his childhood, stuck in the turmoil his parents fed upon like oxygen. Maybe it was because that part of him that wanted her behavior to be a sign of all those deep emotions he should abhor, a sign that she was as overcome by their marriage as he did not wish to admit he was, turned out to be uncannily insistent. Or maybe it took so long because he had become a parody of himself, roaming about his labyrinth like the monster he knew he truly was, deep inside, and counting the hours until she deigned to come home.

That she did so only for sex took him a while to comprehend.

Because one thing was unmistakable. Brita loved sex. She loved every single thing they could do together, her body and his. She was imaginative, inventive, and she adored each and every new thing he'd taught her. There was no *too much*. There was no *enough*.

The only way he could keep her with him was to keep her naked and moaning out her need in his arms.

But even a monster had to sleep, and work, and that was when she slipped back out into the wilderness as if it was her true lover, not him.

Or because that is where she feels safe, that voice in him whispered.

He ignored it.

It was some six weeks after their wedding day when he sat brooding at the dinner table one night, staring with his usual unacknowledged umbrage at his merry wife.

Who had only appeared moments ago, though he had made a point of telling her that he would prefer that they sat down for the evening meal together on the nights they did not have events.

He had told her when he was deep inside her, the only time he could be certain he had her full and focused attention.

She sauntered in looking like a backpacking university student of some sort, with a torn sleeve, what he hoped was mud and not something more ominous smeared across her cheek, and a look of total nonchalance about her.

As if she was not late. As if she was not clearly in from some more extreme and excessive hiking where she could, at any moment, fall to her death.

In remote places where she would never be found, and how would he cope with that?

"This looks lovely." She was beaming down at the platters already crowding the table, all smelling of the sheer local perfection Asterion expected of his personal chef. "I am quite hungry."

It was possible he actually growled. "It would not harm you, I think, to dress for dinner."

Brita shrugged at that. "Or I could undress."

And then she did just that, stripping out of her clothes in that way she had, as if she wasn't attempting to seduce him in any way. As if she simply *preferred* nudity whenever possible and didn't mind if he looked.

She was maddening.

And it was worse when she seated herself at the table in all of her glorious nakedness.

He nearly swallowed his tongue and she barely glanced in his direction.

Asterion had to force himself to concentrate on the extensive list of his grievances, not his enduring lust for this impossible woman.

Because he certainly did not wish to stop and question why it was that his lust for her seemed to have no end. It went on and on, day and night, and only seem to grow sharper, deeper. Bigger. Wider.

Some days it was so large and so intense it was as if he could not breathe through it.

"I would not wish you to mar those perfect breasts by burning them in any way with hot food," he managed to get out with very ill humor. He unbuttoned the shirt he wore and handed it to her, so she could wrap it around her body like a robe.

She looked amused, but she did.

As if any of this was *amusing*.

Then they sat there, staring at each other across the table that had been prepared for them and placed beneath the pergola that was thick with vines not yet in the full bloom and a mess of lights that lit up the whole terrace. Before them was the sea. Behind them, the bedroom they shared and the great tangle of his house, spilling down the cliffside.

But all he could see was her.

Brita smiled at him, all that heat and wickedness in the curve of her mouth, and he wanted to launch himself across the table and get his hands on her. Even as, at the same time, he wanted nothing more than to explain to her why the way she was behaving could not work. Could not be borne.

She must stop this, he told himself, as he often did.

He opened his mouth to tell her so, but stopped himself. Because that eerie realization finally landed, and hard.

All of this was familiar because while *he* was having flashbacks to his childhood and the ways his parents would torment each other, if he ignored that voice inside him, it was obvious that *Brita* was having a different experience entirely.

And he knew that experience well.

She was treating Asterion precisely the way he had always treated his lovers, all throughout his life. She gave her body to him, enthusiastically, delightedly, and without reservation. She talked happily enough about the things she did when she was out there, making her own trail all over the island, much the way he spoke of his work when it was necessary to make polite conversation.

But she did not think about him at all when she was out there, and when she was with him, she was marking time until they could be lost in the flesh and the fever of it all.

No wonder this felt familiar. This was precisely how he had always behaved, as if the women in his life were exercise equipment, however charming.

This, he finally understood, was why they called him a monster.

Asterion could see the irony. He did not know why it bothered him so much. He only knew it did.

"We have been married for six weeks," he told her, in the same dark tone. "And I have told you, almost daily, what my expectations are. Yet you do not heed them."

Brita sat before her still-empty plate, wrapped in his shirt, somehow even lovelier than usual. He wanted to wipe the dirt from her cheek. He wanted to press his mouth to the indentation between her collarbone and her neck. He wanted to kneel before her and lick his way into her soft heat, claiming her and tearing her apart in the only way he could.

"I took a great many vows that day," she said quietly, when he had begun to think that she would not answer him. Though she did not meet his gaze, and he hated that. "But I do not recall agreeing to stop doing the things that bring me joy. On the contrary, I seem to recall *you* promising me that I could continue them. That was the reason I married you."

"That is *one* of the reasons," he could not seem to keep himself from growling.

She shrugged again, but it seemed a jerkier motion than before. As if she was not so nonchalant as she wished to pretend. "I could have called you my temptation and repented at leisure in the convent, Asterion. You know full well I married you so I would not need to give up the hills and the trees and the wild things that live there."

"It is unacceptable," he began, all thunder and doom.

"Why?"

Brita still didn't look at him as she asked this, as if she was so unimpressed with any storm that he might be gathering that she didn't notice—but he couldn't quite believe that. Or maybe he wished to believe it, but she still seemed not quite her nonchalant self. She leaned forward and was helping herself to the food heaped high on the platters before them, but he was sure he saw her hand tremble and her throat convulse, if slightly.

"You are a Teras wife now," he said, though he did not know why he bothered. He had said the same thing many times and it never seemed to land. Not the way he needed it to land. And he did not wish to interrogate this need, only her obstinance. "You knew this when you married me. Whether you like it or not, there are certain expectations of a man in my position."

"And you knew who I was when you asked me to marry you in the first place." She took a bite of the food she'd piled on her plate and did not look at him as she chewed. Then she took her time swallowing. Only then did she shift her gaze to his, the steadiness of it somehow unnerving. Almost as if she was attempting to hide some kind of *hurt* from him— but he rejected that possibility. "Maybe you can explain something to me. Why is it that people seem to think a marriage will change them? Or more to the point, will change the person they've married? You promised me that you would show me where all those kisses went, and you did. I did not expect that you would transform before my eyes. I don't understand why you thought that I would."

"Because I asked you to."

Her sun and moon eyes seemed perhaps too wise as she gazed back at him. Or perhaps it was something else—but he rejected that, too. "Did you ask me such a thing?"

"Every day," he threw at her.

She studied him. "You have thundered on about a great many things and I have assumed that you simply wished to express those things into the ether. Because if people talk to me like that, I ignore them. And you know this. I was sneaking in and out of my own father's house because I was tired of having similar conversations with him. Why would you think I would behave any differently now?"

"I know you are not comparing me to your father."

"What has changed since our wedding?" Brita was still looking at him, too intently, as if he was a puzzle to solve. He disliked it. He was no such thing. He was made entirely of reason and logic. "Why are you so determined to exert your control?"

"It is not about exerting control. It is about safety. Security. And like it or not, the Teras legacy itself." But he found he did not care for the way those familiar words sat so bitterly on his tongue tonight.

"I've stood with you on hillsides bathed in the magic of the sky, watching the sunset, with no other thought in my head." She shook her head at him. "Why would you think I would give that up? Why would you want to give it up yourself?"

"There are standards," he told her. But he couldn't understand what was happening inside him. He felt as if something in him was tearing apart, ripping wide-open at the seams, though that made no sense. "We are *married* now."

Brita only looked at him in that same, sad way that got deep beneath his skin. "So you keep reminding me."

And inside him, those fragile seams broke.

"The man I was willing to pretend I was while getting to know you is not the man I am," he hurled at her, aware as he did that he was aiming for her as surely as she'd aimed that arrow of hers at him. He intended it to land. "The man I am has a certain station in life. And there are a set of expectations that go along with that. Not the world's expectations, Brita.

Mine. I could not change that if I wanted to, and I do not want to. This is who I am."

He expected her to go pale. To blanch at his words, and the truth he had not imagined he would need to tell her—that the man she'd met and spoken to in the moonlight was not him at all.

But instead, this confounding wife of his merely gazed at him, steady and sure.

And less sad than before.

"I never pretended to be someone else," she said, quiet and direct. "So if someone must change now that we are married, Asterion, I don't see why it would be me."

And when he started to argue the point, she simply stood and slipped out of the shirt given her, so she was naked before him once again. Because he'd taught her how to use these weapons, and she did. Oh, how joyfully she used them.

Tonight she took it nuclear, sinking down onto her knees before him.

And no matter how many times he told himself he would not, could not, lose his head with these games she played, he couldn't seem to help it.

All she had to do was look at him with that fire in her eyes.

Then touch him—with her hands, her mouth, her flesh pressed to his.

So easily, every time, he was lost.

And it never mattered, in those moments, that he knew better. It never mattered what promises he'd made to himself. It never mattered that he'd vowed that he would not allow her to make him little more than cannon fodder.

Much later, after they'd torn each other apart again and again, on the terrace and in the bedroom and then again in the great shower in their suite, he watched her brush out her long, raven black hair.

Even when she did not mean to be a sensual feast for his eyes, she was.

All she had to do was breathe and his gaze began to trace her perfect form, from her lush breasts to her tiny waist, to the flare of her hips—

But tonight, something else dawned on him.

"You're staring at me again," she said, though her eyes were soft when they found his in the mirror. She did not stop her brushing. "The casual observer might conclude that for all your brooding, you quite like me."

"Brita." But something else dawned on him. "It's been six weeks."

"So you keep reminding me, when you must realize I care little about time. I prefer to count seasons."

He ignored that nonsense with the strength of his purpose and his dawning suspicion. "We have been together every day, usually several times a day."

"We have."

She smiled then, in that way she did sometimes, so smug and satisfied that she made him hard all over again.

He did not usually let that pass without taking the opportunity to make her sob out his name a few times, as penance.

Tonight he had something else working in him. Call it forewarning. Or a premonition. Or perhaps a simple, deep *knowing,* in the way he sometimes knew things. He usually called it instinct, though this felt far more primitive than that. "Yet you have not bled."

She blinked, and her hands slowed in her hair. She let the brush drop to her lap and looked down at it, and her voice sounded odd when she replied. "No. I have not. I don't know why I didn't notice that before now."

And what washed over him, through him, then was far more complicated than simple triumph, or even fear.

Though in the moment, it felt like *light.*

He strode to the door of the bedroom and bellowed out an order.

And so it was that within the hour, there was a test at the door, and an answer.

She was pregnant. Brita was *pregnant.*

His wife was pregnant with his child, the heir to his fortune and his half of the Teras estate.

And that meant that Asterion was done playing games.

CHAPTER TEN

BRITA HAD NEVER thought about being a mother.

Her own mother had been such a nonevent in her life, notable only for her absence, and she'd always thought of the island itself as the true maternal influence in her life. Maybe it made sense that, having never wanted to marry in the first place, it had never occurred to her to consider what it might be like to have her own children.

After all, there were so many creatures who needed her.

But all it took were two blue lines on a stick and she rather thought that motherhood sounded like exactly the kind of magical experience she could get behind.

Besides, she had always liked baby creatures of any description. Surely she would love her own even more.

Brita knew she would. She knew instantly. She felt all the love she'd kept inside her expand and glow every time she thought of the baby. And every time she thought of the baby's father. She felt herself grow big and swollen with it, all that love, when her body had yet to change much at all.

She was *ripening* with all that terrible, wonderful, marvelous love that seemed to weave its way into her bones until she felt that even the way she walked and talked and *breathed* was different. And she might not have known much love from people in her life, but she could no longer be afraid of it. She could no longer run away from it.

Because this time it was happening from the inside out, an earthquake that went on and on and on.

It was beautiful. It was so magically, marvelously *perfect*.

But she did not share these thoughts with her husband.

Not that night, when he went thin lipped and glittery eyed.

And not in the days that followed, when everything changed. And not just inside her.

Suddenly there was more staff, everywhere. And more requests from them for her thoughts on domestic affairs that interested her not at all. When she woke up in the morning, she was greeted at the door of the bedroom by happy, smiling members of Asterion's heretofore unseen staff, who would chatter at her as they led her from one thing to the next. There were wardrobe fittings, which were tedious. There were social calls, which were even more tedious, and worse, usually involved the kind of arch, snide conversation that she had always disliked the most.

It reminded her too much of treacherous evenings

in the Martis villa, trying to make herself invisible while her family sniped on all around her, sinking deeper and deeper into their cups and gripes and endless conspiracies.

Brita had made herself into a woman she could admire, who knew how to use a bow. She saw her target and she shot it. She did not dance around it, using innuendo or a perfectly placed rolled eye instead of the words she meant.

These social calls reminded her of too many forced interactions with her stepmother, and if she'd wanted that, she could have stayed in the villa instead of escaping to the convent and the far reaches of the island.

But it was not until they were driving back up the drive one night, not long after she'd taken that pregnancy test, that she realized that there was a method to all of this that she'd missed. Likely because she was used to being required to do things she did not wish to do by people who were chaotic, if single-minded.

Of course, Asterion did not have the same goals that her family had always had for her.

"Has a threat been made against you?" she asked Asterion in the car.

"There are always threats," he replied, which was not an answer.

But she understood then. He was being nicer about it. He was neither drunk nor disorderly. It was wrapped up in elegance and requests for her opinions and yet in the end, Asterion was doing exactly the same thing that her family had done back in the day.

He was attempting to imprison her.

And unlike back then, she was letting him.

Because when he touched her, it felt like magic. And she had found so little magic in her life, where people were concerned. She wanted to bask in it longer. She wanted to tell herself stories about why he was behaving the way he did.

She spent hours trying to build good reasons for everything he did, to convince herself. That legacy of his, like a rope held taut around his neck. His grandmother's interference in his affairs, however well-meant.

The tragedy of losing his parents so young.

Brita tried and she tried.

But later that night she waited for him to fall asleep beside her, as he always did. And then, even though she took such a deep, intense pleasure in curling her body up with his and breathing him in as she slept, she got up.

Because she had to.

Because there was something inside her, like a drumbeat, letting her know that if she did not—if she let herself be swallowed up in whatever this was he was doing—she would not emerge whole.

It turned out that there could be too much feeling, and she thought she might succumb to it entirely if she didn't *move*.

For the first time in her life, she thought that perhaps, she understood her own mother's need to run a little.

She dressed silently and then set about seeking her way past the new set of guards he had imported for this new phase of his. Brita moved quietly and carefully, aware that the kind of guards that Asterion was likely to hire were obviously going to be better trained than her own drunken family members.

Still, it was quite late when she finally made it into the hills she loved, collected her bow from the place where she normally stashed it, and felt Heracles lean once more against her legs.

He panted a little. The stars were bright.

Brita told herself she was content.

She did her usual rounds and told herself that, too, was as it always had been. And that it was good. She decided it was fine with her if things were as they'd been when she'd been nominally a resident of her father's house. At least this way, she could carry on making her own world as she liked it.

Every night then, she waited as Asterion fell asleep beside her. She dressed silently and amused herself with various escapes from the house, thankful for her years of tracking wild animals that, it turned out, made her excellent at avoiding guards.

Who, in fairness, were more focused on keeping people out than keeping her in.

Or so she assumed.

She assured herself that she could live a whole life like this, close enough to perfectly happy—or closer than she'd ever been when her family were involved in her daily life. But when she would find herself cupping her belly, wondering about the child she carried, she would very carefully not think about how this would work when there was a baby in the mix. Because though she might have come to a place of peace when it came to thoughts about her own mother, she did not intend to act like her mother had.

Over my dead body, she thought instead.

And then, one night, she found herself out on that same viewpoint where Asterion had once joined her.

Maybe she'd been avoiding it.

Because it was here where the moon sat high above the sea and looked as if it was making a silvery pathway across the water, she had to face a fact she'd been avoiding.

It just wasn't the same.

When she'd snuck away from the old Martis villa, she'd felt her burdens disappear the moment the dark welcomed her into its embrace. She had felt free and unfettered. The hills had felt like home, before the convent and even more during the last year. She didn't think about her family or their demands at all while she was out in the hills.

But these days, no matter what she was doing out here, the only thing she could think about was Asterion.

It was maddening.

She went and sat out on the edge of the cliffs, the way she always had. She stared out at the sea, which she had used to do for hours, and all she could see was Asterion.

Asterion with his head thrown back, taking his pleasure in her body and sweeping her right along with him. Asterion laughing the way he had in those early days, out here with her, though he never did that any longer. Him smiling in that way he had that every nun she knew would call sinful, that lit every single part of her on fire.

And Asterion the night they had discovered she was pregnant.

You will be a mother, he had told her, sounding grimmer than she had ever heard him, while she was still trying to wrestle with all the many emotions fighting for purchase inside her. *That changes everything.*

Perhaps, she had replied, still trying to take in the news. And the notion that she was carrying a new life *inside* of her. *But not for many months.*

And he had looked at her as if she had betrayed him.

As if she had struck him with one of her arrows in truth, piercing him to the bone.

Brita did not like it at all when Asterion looked at her like that.

It would be the same as if Heracles, panting softly beside her, suddenly turned his head and snapped his teeth in her direction.

She would feel...hurt, yes. But she would wonder if he was hurt, too, that he should act so unlike himself.

She frowned, no longer seeing the glorious view

before her because all she could seem to concentrate on now was Asterion.

Every member of her family had accused her of betraying them at one point or another, and she had never cared at all. Because she hadn't, and she didn't think they believed most of the absurd things they said anyway. Asterion had not accused her of anything at all, yet here she was, all these days later, still worrying that moment over and over in her head.

And none of her made-up stories helped her feel any better.

She blew out a breath, and wondered why everything couldn't be as simple as it seemed when they were both naked together. That was when everything felt like music. That was when every part of her seemed to work in perfect concert with every part of him.

As if they had been put on this earth to make such songs together that it could put the moon and sun to shame.

She suddenly understood all those mournful tracks the people she knew at university had played in the pubs when they were feeling maudlin. All the conversations she'd overheard in those days that she hadn't been able to make any sense of, knowing as little as she did of men. Or sex.

Or all these inconvenient *feelings*.

Even when he was at his darkest, smirkiest, and grimmest, all she wanted was to put her hands on him. To be near him. Not only to have sex with him, though it was true that she adored that.

It had used to be the only time she knew peace was when she was out in these hills.

But here she was, right now, and she didn't feel at peace at all. What she longed to do, instead, was go back to his house and twine herself around him once more. Because sleeping with him felt safe. Warm.

Like home, something in her whispered.

The sex was like dessert. And Brita had always liked dessert. But it was the *home* part that made her ache...

And everything in her shifted as the implications of that seemed to wind their way into her, because she'd never really had a home. Thinking of him that way felt the way the moonlight did, dancing over the water, making a bridge—

And that was when she knew.

All that love that ripened within her. All that love that infused her with light. All that *love* was not just for the baby she carried.

How had she missed the truth of it?

She was in love with him.

She was in love with him, she thought in amazement, as the words bubbled up inside of her like joy. She must have made some noise because Heracles whined softly, then trailed behind her as she leaped to her feet and started back for the house.

Because she could not exist a moment more without sharing this extraordinary news with the one person it affected most.

It was so *huge*. It made everything make sense.

It made it easy to turn around and run toward him rather than away.

It was why he felt like home.

The only home she'd ever had.

Surely, Brita thought, this was what had been missing all along.

How marvelous that she could fix it now that she'd figured it out. And maybe Asterion might find his way back to the man he'd been when she'd met him. He could tell her he'd been pretending, but she'd been there. And she knew liars and pretenders better than she'd have preferred. He wasn't one of them.

Maybe he'd felt as free out there as she always had. Maybe they could find it again, together.

Brita didn't bother slinking back in the labyrinth, covered in stealth and shadows. She stowed her bow and arrow in the trees where she always did and then walked onto the grounds of Asterion's grand estate, smiling when the guards surrounded her. She raised her hands over her head while Heracles howled out his disapproval in the distance, such a dangerous sound it made the men look around as if a pack of wolves might come tearing over the cliff at any moment.

There was a great deal of radioing and muttering into mouthpieces, and the men escorted her—a bit dramatically, she thought—into the glass dome of light. Only then did they leave her to descend the great central stair by herself.

This was a house of many stairs and she loved them all. But this one was her favorite, as it wound around and around, all the way down to the very lowest level of the house, like something lovely floating down toward the sea, buoyed by the breeze. And she was still learning the ins and outs of this new home of hers. The place was a kind of inevitable slide of glass-enclosed rooms with steel girders that led inexorably down to the wing of the tangled labyrinth where Asterion plotted out how to rule more of the world. A pageant of power, someone at one of the endless parade of parties had murmured in her hearing.

But the spiral stair felt like art, not commerce. Walking on it felt like soaring, dancing, all decked in light.

She floated down one level into the next, around and around, until she reached the level she knew best. The sprawling bedroom and living area, where Asterion was waiting for her.

Dark and grim, as if he was actively attempting to black out everything else.

But she knew the moon better than he did, didn't she?

Brita glanced back up the stair, but the guards were nowhere in sight. She stopped moving a few steps up from where he waited and looked down at Asterion.

This man she had married. This man she had let inside her body. This man who had made a child with her.

This man she wondered if she'd loved all along, ever since she'd looked up to see him appear like a dream in the door to the villa's old kitchen. A dream that felt like one she'd had forever, never seeing his face.

Until he walked in and it was as if she'd never seen anything but that face.

Tonight he looked as if he'd risen directly from the bed, and only moments ago. He looked as close to *rumpled* as she had ever seen him, his dark hair defying his usual insistence that it resemble a military evenness, and that was all the evidence she could need that he was not quite himself.

There was also that betrayed look about him again. She hated that.

And in case Brita had any doubt, it made her heart hurt to look at him. She wanted to run to him. She wanted to throw herself into his arms—

She would have, she nearly did, but something about the way he studied her stopped her. It held her fast where she stood, as if she was facing down a creature with teeth and a terrible wound out there in the dark.

"You are leaving me no choice," he gritted out to her, his voice like gravel. "You cannot leave your protection to chance."

Her heart ached in her chest, even as it worked overtime, and she felt overripe and bruised with the need to tell him all of the feelings that she'd discovered.

But she paused at that.

"Protection?" she asked softly. "Surely you are

aware that I have been protecting myself for a very long time, Asterion."

He seemed to grow darker. Grimmer. "Things are different now, little as you seem able to accept it. You carry not only my name, my child, but the heir to everything I have built and half of everything my family has made."

She wanted to laugh, because why should any of those things matter when the world waited *right there* on the other side of that glass? When there were flowers that only bloomed at night that most people never knew were there? Wonders required the freedom to explore them, not locked up rooms and guards on the perimeter, no matter how many windows he'd built to let the light in.

It wasn't the same.

Why didn't he want to give their child those things?

"I will protect that heir, and *my* child, and I suppose your name as well, the same way I have protected myself." She smiled, though it felt fake. Like it belonged on the face of one of those women at her wedding, or the parties he took her to. As if she wanted the smile to *do something,* instead of simply letting it be what it was. "Or have you forgotten that I'm the one who pinned you to a tree and could have done much worse?"

"I haven't forgotten anything." But it sounded like an accusation.

"I don't understand any of this."

Brita drifted down another step. She studied

him, standing there before her in all of his masculine splendor. He had not bothered to do more than throw on a pair of trousers. They were unbuttoned, there over his narrow hips where that flat, low, furred plane below his navel made her feel shivery. All the rest of him was the same golden shade and it was all more of that lean, whipcord strength that defined him.

She had put her mouth on almost every part of this man, and she still hungered for more. He'd been inside her only hours ago, and yet she felt empty, needy.

She'd never felt such greed in her life.

"I have told you," Asterion said in that low, *betrayed* sort of voice. "I have told you time and again, Brita. This is not a *request*. Things cannot continue as they have. You certainly cannot keep up these... childish pursuits of yours. You can either do as I have asked or be swept up in it anyway. The choice is yours, but I promise you, this gallivanting about, risking yourself and *our child,* is at an end."

She wanted to lash out at that, and she nearly did, but she had grown up in a hard school. She knew better. And besides, she didn't want to argue with him, no matter what bizarre things he was saying.

Brita was more interested in why he was acting like this, but she didn't think he'd tell her if she asked.

Because she had asked. And asked.

So instead, she told him the only thing that really mattered. "Tonight I sat on the edge of the cliff where you and I once stood together. It's where I go to think of nothing but the beauty of this island and the world. But I realized you are the only thing I could think about."

He did not look as if there were tides of joy inside him, yearning to break free, at that statement.

She tried again. "I realized that nothing else, and no one else, has ever intruded on my time in the wilderness."

Brita really thought he might understand then, but he only stared back at her, his gaze dark and opaque.

She sighed. "I love you, Asterion."

And she expected everything to change then, the way it had when he'd kissed her. When everything had been turned on its head and nothing was as it had been before.

She expected it would feel the same—that sudden, shocking acknowledgment that her life was not at all what she'd thought it was. That all the while, there had been another truth waiting for her, just out of reach.

But if anything, he looked as if those words... *hurt* him.

As if she might as well have bitten him and sunk her teeth in deep until she found the bone.

For the first time, possibly ever, Brita did not feel steady on her own two feet.

"That is the worst thing you could possibly have said to me," he told her, as if he was a man condemned. There was nothing but dread all over him. It was in his voice. It was in that gaze of his. She could feel it, hanging all around her like a heavy cloak. "You might as well have consigned us to our doom. I hope you're happy."

Brita felt the way she thought it must feel to be on the receiving end of one of her own arrows—steel shot straight through the heart, an inarguable death sentence.

She didn't know how she was still standing.

She didn't know why she could still draw breath.

And Brita had always thought that dead things died on impact, but here she was. Still upright. Still breathing no matter how little she wished to. She could still feel her pulse in her veins.

She could still feel exactly how much those words had hurt.

"Do you hear me?" he asked then, ruthlessly, and at least that was different. There was a little more heat in his voice then, even as he glared at her. "I promised you endless kisses and sex. And a wildlife refuge. It was never meant to be about *love*. Ever. That is the bargain we made."

"But the bargain has changed," she heard herself say, when she had no plan to speak.

She felt as if she was acting on some kind of auto-pilot when she was used to being a woman of intention and focus—or maybe it was simply that there was no need to pretend. There was no need for anything but these deep truths she hadn't even known were inside her.

Having never loved anyone before in her life, not a human anyway, it wasn't that she'd expected it to be *easy*. Maybe it was always hard. Maybe it always made you feel as if love and grief were the same, depending on the moment.

But it wasn't as if she could go back and *unsay* it. Much less *unfeel* it.

"I have changed," she clarified. "You have changed me. There's no going back, Asterion. I couldn't go back if I wanted to, and I don't. I won't."

"Then you're doomed," he told her in that same voice of dark and dread, as if he was delivering them both a life sentence. "And you might as well consider yourself in prison, Brita, because you are. Until such a time as you come to your senses."

CHAPTER ELEVEN

FOR A MOMENT she looked devastated, and it nearly killed him.

But Asterion decided that he must have imagined it.

Because her chin tilted up. Something that looked like battle blazed in her eyes.

She was every inch the huntress of his wildest fantasies.

So it was his own perversities—his not so inner monster, he supposed—that made him almost wish that she really had been devastated by him. That he could reach her that way.

What kind of man was he to wish such a thing on his own wife?

"I am not the one who needs to come to her senses," she said after a moment, and there was a huskiness in her voice, but no other hint that she was discussing anything more emotionally fraught than the endlessly beautiful weather. "You can imprison me for a thousand years, Asterion. I will love you all the while." She inclined her head then, just slightly. "I will also try to murder you, but I'm beginning to understand that those two things can be the same, if necessary."

"*You cannot love me*," he thundered at her then, the words coming from some terrible place deep within him. "I forbid it."

And when she laughed, it was as if something simply crumbled into ash inside of him. It was like losing himself all over again. It was like the sudden, shocking impact, steel against steel, the jolting and the rolling, and then waking into horror.

It was like a darkness that spread through him, eating everything whole and spinning him around again.

"You cannot forbid me to do anything," she was telling him, still laughing, when nothing had ever been less funny. "I'm your wife. Not one of your domestic staff. Or one of your little corporate underlings. *I* do not race about, desperate for your approval. It does not matter to *me* if you issue lists upon lists of orders. I will only follow them if I wish to." Her laughter faded, and her gaze were something like solemn. "I'm sorry if you don't like it. But not sorry enough to act as if I work for you, or anyone."

"You need to listen to me," he growled, and then he was advancing on her, though surely he should know better by now. There was nothing to be gained by putting his hands on her and too much to lose, but he did it.

There was that heat, as always. There was that terrible longing. There was the sure knowledge that he was already in too deep with her—but wasn't that the trouble? She was quicksand and he couldn't fight his way out, but he kept trying.

Because he was determined that this marriage would end better than his parents had.

There was a part of him, that terrible monster that he knew lurked within him, that understood things he had always condemned. Like seeing his father shake his mother. Was that the near-electric urge that raced through him then? Was that why his skin prickled? Did he want to simply cross that line once and for all and stop pretending he could make himself any better?

Besides, he doubted very much that Brita would respond the way his mother had, merely issuing a ringing slap before falling into his father's arms. Kissing him madly until the two of them had started shouting at each other all over again, because such was the carousel they lived on. Such was the ride everyone near them was forced to partake in, like it or not.

But none of that mattered. What mattered was that he felt the urge at all.

This was why he had always lived his life so committed to keeping such tight control of everything. His feelings. His thoughts. The whole of his world.

Because he knew.

The intensity in his blood led to darkness and death.

He had witnessed it himself.

"This thing between us is like a fever," he growled.

She dared to look amused. "You told me it was nothing of the kind."

"It is like a fever, we are both infected, and you think that we can survive this, Brita, but I know better." He gripped her, not hard, and even that felt like a bridge too far over a very old, very dark abyss. "I know where this ends. It will consume us whole."

She did not fight him. She did not pull away. She melted into him, her eyes imploring on his. "Isn't it supposed to?"

"It is like a cancer," he seethed at her. "You can try this therapy or that, but it always gets worse. It always grows bigger. And then, soon enough, you become heedless of your surroundings. Incapable of controlling yourself. Your evil lies inside you, until it explodes, and it will. It always does. And there's no telling who we will take with us when we go."

There was some new shine in her eyes then, making them more silver than gold, as if she needed to be more luminous. "I don't understand."

He wanted to shout, to throw things through walls, to shatter all the glass in this house.

But that was why he had built this house *of* glass. So that he couldn't risk that kind of tantrum. So that he couldn't start behaving the way his parents had, unless he wished to fall off into the sea with the shards.

Asterion fought to remember who he was.

It was distressingly difficult.

He forced himself to step back. "My parents called their relationship *tempestuous*. But in reality, it was torture. They tortured each other, day in and day out. There were always accusations, fights, shouting matches. They threw vases at each other's heads. They threw furniture through windows. They screamed and cried and clawed at each other, and then they called it passion and disappeared into the bedroom for days, and this rolled into everything. It consumed them whole, and then us, too."

Brita searched his face. "I assure you, there were no relationships in the house I grew up in that anyone would wish to emulate. But that doesn't mean—"

"They were in one of their fights," he gritted out, because he couldn't seem to stop himself. He never told this story. He had lived it, and then there were the versions the media liked to spin, and he'd never spoken of it to anyone but his brother, in the most oblique terms. "Poseidon and I were twelve. We waited with our grandfather for them, in the foyer of the house my grandmother still claims, and we all stood there listening to the splintering of furniture above. When they came down, they were both glittery eyed and disheveled, and it was never easy to tell what, exactly they had been doing. All of their passions had a price, you see. They called their bruises *souvenirs*."

Brita only seemed to melt into him more, when she wasn't even touching him just then.

Asterion regretted that he had ever started down the path of this story, but he couldn't seem to stop. "My father insisted on driving. My mother soundly abused him for this arrogance because she preferred to take a car with a driver, so that she could have my father's full attention. Perhaps you remember the road down from my grandmother's house, with all its twists and turns." Brita nodded, and he swallowed. He found his throat appallingly dry, but even this did not stop him. "In the rain, it is treacherous. But they were too busy shouting at each other to care. As always."

Brita looked something like sad. Terribly sad, and she lifted a hand, as if to touch him—but he couldn't allow that. "Asterion…"

"We were all in the car when it took the last curve too fast to see the sedan coming in the opposite direction. There was no possibility of avoiding the impact. Someone screamed, I remember that."

She whispered his name again.

That helped. He had forgotten the screaming—he wanted to forget it again, and how it had been choked off so abruptly. He swallowed again. "Somehow, Poseidon and I survived. But we had the bad luck of remembering our parents as they were, not as they were eulogized. And there was never any doubt that the same demons lurked within us. We both vowed that we would never become what they were."

"You cannot think…" she began, frowning.

"I had no worries on that score, Brita," he gritted out at her. "I enjoy sex. I like women. It is only you that has made me doubt my own control. Only you that has made me wonder if all this time, I have been lying to myself."

"About something that happened when you were twelve years old? And are in no way responsible?"

He felt something else snap, deep inside, as if it was a fragile thing he had been hiding all along.

"Don't you see?" he demanded. "I have always been destined to be the very same monster. The reality of me is as dark and as twisted as the people who made me. The Monster of the Mediterranean is no joke. It is who I am. This man you see? This Asterion Teras, who has made such a name for himself? This has always been a mask."

That was far more difficult to say than perhaps it should have been.

Still, it was the truth, no matter how unwelcome. His chest hurt, as if he'd run straight up the side of a mountain. Everything hurt, he realized, as if he was waking up in that mangled mess of a car again—but the only thing he could seem to do was keep his gaze trained on Brita.

Who for some reason did not look as horrified as she should.

If anything, her eyes were soft.

Soft enough that something in him seemed to sing out in response—

But then she lifted her chin in that same belligerent way of hers that he could not understand why he found so alluring. The next moment, her eyes were not soft at all.

Instead, she simply gazed back at him, challenge written all over her.

"Take it off then," she said.

He felt all the wind leave his body. "I beg your pardon?"

She waved a hand in a manner so peremptory that it reminded him of his grandmother. "Take it off," she said again. She made a low noise. "I want both, Asterion. The monster as well as the man. Don't you see? I want everything."

Something in him jumped at that, painfully, but he could not allow it. He could not permit anything that felt like hope when he had already lived through the wreckage of a relationship like this once. The literal wreckage. He could not do it again.

"You should run from this, from me. I mean it, Brita. It can only end in disaster." He hated saying these things. It was as if his own body rebelled as he spoke. But he forced himself to keep going. "You should take our child and go to one of those wild places you love so much, where I can never find you."

But Brita only laughed.

And this time, she tossed her head back, as if calling down the gods of old to laugh with her.

Asterion couldn't decide if he was thrilled or incensed. It didn't seem to matter. It hurt him and he wanted her all the same.

"If I run," she said, tilting her head slightly to one side, "will you catch me? Or will I catch you in the end?"

Something in him began to beat, low and hard, like a drum.

"That's not what I meant at all."

She moved then, putting her face entirely too close to his. "Because if I do catch you, there will be a cost to you, *agapi mu*. And of the two of us, I have to say that I like my chances when it comes to a hunt."

"I don't have the slightest idea what you're talking about. There is no *hunt,* Brita."

But if that was true, why did he feel a strange, new kind of lightning inside of him at the thought?

"You have hunted me from the start," she said. "And I have hunted you in return. But we have circled around each other all the while, pretending we were not doing the very thing we have been doing all along. What if we both stopped pretending?"

Asterion thought his heartbeat was so loud it might shatter the windows.

"You cannot take such a risk," he growled.

And he saw something crack then, there on her lovely face. He could see, for a dizzying sort of moment, that this was far harder for her than he had imagined. That she *felt* all these storms just as he did.

That neither one of them was alone in this.

But then she blinked, and the light of battle was back.

As if she knew, somehow, he needed a challenge, not a cuddle. Not when the monster in him was in control.

"If I win," she told him, very deliberately, her gaze steady, "I win you. All of you."

This was not what Asterion had intended. He didn't even know what this was.

But he did know one thing. He was not a man accustomed to losing. And somehow, all his talk of cancers and fevers seemed to wrap up and tangle inside him, then wash away as he got closer to her, too.

"You cannot win," he growled at her. "You won't."

They stayed like that for far too long, suspended in the force of the way they gazed at each other. Asterion wasn't sure which one of them was breathing heavily—he only knew that he could hear it.

He could very nearly taste it.

Brita let her smile flash like quicksilver, there for an instant, then gone.

"I wish you good luck," she said, as formally as a vow. Then she laughed again. "You will need it."

Before he could process those words, she whirled around and was gone. Flying back up that stair, moving faster than should have been possible.

And he was so stunned that, for moment, he simply...watched.

It was a sight that would be stamped into his bones for the rest of his life. He knew this too well. His huntress, his Brita, charging up the stairs at full speed, all that thick and inky hair streaming behind her like a train.

He had the presence of mind to call off his guards, but then he took after her.

He assumed she would head straight up toward the entrance to the house, but she didn't. She feinted left, then took a hard right, running through this house he'd built as if she knew it better than he did.

Then it was like they were both lost in the same maze. A maze he had created and should have known like the back of his own hands, but it was different tonight.

It was different because he felt haunted by the woman he saw only in glimpses as they both ran. She was a little bit here, a little bit there. When he thought he had her cornered, there was only the impression of her on an empty landing.

There was the sound of her laughter down a curving hall. There was her reflection, always dancing away, out of reach.

It was almost as if he'd made her up.

Yet as he hit one dead end after another, he never once thought of giving up. Or letting her run off as she liked.

As she should.

Because he was Asterion Teras. He did not give up. He won.

No matter what, he won—

But still it felt like something of a relief when he saw her start back to the grand spiral stair and finally rush for the glass globe that would lead her to the outdoors.

He did not stop to think. He did not question himself.

He burst out into the night and he charged for her, chasing her as she ran flat out for the woods that lurked on the far side of the cliff.

Then the game began again in earnest.

And here, in these hills where Brita had always been a part of the same wilderness that surrounded him now on all sides, Asterion felt the last vestiges of the man he'd tried so hard to become fall away.

Until there was nothing left but *this*.

His feet against the earth. The pounding of his heart. The heat in his sex and the fire in his blood and her name all over him, like rain.

And this was no car crash. This was no tempest. This was elemental. This was blood and bone.

She was the song the night sang around him, otherworldly and astonishing, and most of all, his.

I love you, she had said. And had meant it. He had seen that she meant it.

And somehow, this hunt of theirs, this game that wasn't a game at all, seemed to bring those words into him with every breath.

With every step, and her laughter on the breeze, she loved him.

She loved him, and she hadn't said it that first night, after the kiss. The way women had before, angling for his money, his fame.

She hadn't said it at their wedding, when anyone might have been swept away by the vows and the pageantry.

She hadn't said it on their wedding night, when he'd made her sob over and over again as he'd taught her things about her body she hadn't known.

Instead, she'd said it tonight.

When he'd been nothing but dark and grim for weeks.

She'd said it, knowing full well that she carried his child, and if she wished, she could take him for his fortune and his protection for at least the next eighteen years.

Because she had not only signed all those documents he'd put before her, he had watched as she'd read each and every one of them.

She loved him, and still they ran.

Again and again, he nearly caught her—but only nearly.

And he began to feel that she knew all of this too well. Not just the island they raced through, though she was clearly a part of it in a way he never would be. It was as if they had danced this dance before.

Brita had somehow navigated his own maze better than him. And now they were out here, in these hills she knew better than most knew their own bedrooms, and she was nimble and fleet of foot.

Every now and again he saw the shadow of that wolf of hers, always at his flank, but never attacking him.

Asterion had to think that meant something.

He could not have said how long they played this game. But finally, as perhaps he'd always known they would, they ended up on that same cliff once again, where they had once watched the moon like a ladder over the sea.

The cliff where, she had only told him earlier tonight, she had understood she was in love with him.

And now he knew that he had never wanted anything more, in all his life, than to hear her say those words again.

He chased her out into the clearing, then stopped,

because when she turned to face him, she was holding that bow.

"You won't shoot me," he said, in a low, thick voice he did not recognize as his own.

As if the monster had taken him over at last, but tonight he could not seem to mind that as he should.

"Wrong again," Brita murmured.

And then, even as he took a breath to order her to stop, she let loose the arrow.

He felt the impact a scant moment later.

It punched at him, knocking him off his feet until he found himself flat on his back.

Asterion waited for the searing pain. For the agony to catch up with him, and the strangest part was, he couldn't even blame her—

But the pain didn't come.

Brita did.

She moved over him and stood above him, another arrow notched into her bow as she looked down at him. He saw the steel of her gaze and the curve of her lips, and then another arrow flew.

Asterion didn't flinch, and he thought he deserved far more congratulations for that than he received.

For a moment, he thought that maybe it was the power of that gaze of hers, sun and moon together, that made him imagine he wasn't wounded.

But when she lowered her bow and he tried to test what was left of his body, he understood.

She'd shot the arrow at his hips, but not to his

flesh. Each one hammered straight into the ground, right on the seams of the loose trousers he wore.

Pinning him there, unless he wished to tear off his trousers and rise.

Which he might have done, but Brita still stood there above him. She considered him for a moment, then tossed her bow and her quiver to the side.

As he watched, she smiled at him and shrugged out of her clothes. One garment after the next, revealing herself to him with that efficiency that made his sex pound with need.

When she was naked, she moved to kneel between his legs and looked up at him, her naked skin gleaming like marble in the moonlight.

But he knew better. He knew exactly how warm she was, how soft and supple.

"I love you," she told him, almost sternly. "And better yet, I have won you. You are mine now, Asterion Teras, *agapi mu*. For as long as we both shall live. And you will not imprison me. Or this child. Or any other children we have. We will all run wild when we like, and we will go into society and put on our masks when we must, but all the while we will know, deep in our hearts, who we really are."

"Brita," he grated out, "I don't want to hurt you."

"I don't intend to let you," she whispered back.

She reached out between them and freed him from his trousers, torn as they were. And the first thing she did was lean down and take him in her mouth, licking him long and sweet and deep.

Because he had taught her, she knew how to tease him. How to make him groan and sink his fists in her hair.

She brought him to the edge again and again, until he would have pierced his own flesh with one of her damned arrows if she would just—

But she eased back and studied him, looking entirely too pleased with her handiwork.

"Brita…" he managed to say, but it sounded like a wild thing.

And she took far too long for his liking, but she smiled. Then she climbed up onto him and settled herself there, taking the laziest route imaginable before sinking down on him, taking him deep into her heat.

"I already know you love me," she whispered as she rocked her hips and made him see stars. "I suspect I'm the only woman you have ever chased, both in service to your grandmother and tonight. There is only one reason why you would do such a thing."

"Brita—" he growled.

"And you will tell me, soon enough," she told him, and her eyes were narrow as she worked herself over him, but he could see the sun and the moon and all that heat. "Because I will not imprison you, either. And I will always see you, no matter what you wear. We will stand in stuffy ballrooms where no one eats and everyone drinks too much, and everything is fake and brittle, and I will know exactly how wild you are, deep within you, where only I get to see it."

"Brita," he managed to get out. "I—"

"I already know," she told him, there beneath the stars.

And he knew then.

He did not need to control her. She did not need to run.

They needed this.

The magic here. The moon.

The two of them, when the chase was done, right back where they'd begun.

Freedom was what they found together. Love was what they made it. Passion was only dangerous when it turned toxic, and they could control that without having to control each other.

She was no myth and he was no monster. They were flesh and blood.

And they belonged together, just like this.

Brita took him straight out into the cosmos then, in a glorious rush that he could do nothing at all to stop, and the truth was, he didn't want to.

And all the while he whispered, "I am yours, my huntress. I am yours forever."

The second time he said it, there in her ear, after he took his time returning her the favor of that tease. That torment.

A torment that made them shatter, but nothing else.

And the third time, he shouted it.

So loud that later, Brita would swear the moon shouted it right back. That night, and every night after.

CHAPTER TWELVE

EVERYTHING REALLY DID change that night, and Asterion was glad of it.

It wasn't that he stopped being who he was, protective and overbearing and occasionally grim and stern straight through, as his wife had no trouble pointing out to him. But the core of who they were had changed because of that hunt. Because of that moon.

Because she had loved him enough to fight for him.

And every day that passed that led into months, that turned into years, there was a little less despair in him. And a little more joy.

Because he loved her enough to fight for them.

After she delivered him one perfect daughter, as wild as her mother though named for his grandmother—who inclined her head as if accepting an expected tribute, then wiped away a tear from her cheek—they decided it was time to look for the refuge she wanted.

But it quickly became clear that there was one such place already, and it had been taken over by the wilderness already. And so even though Asterion had paid off her family when he'd married her, and given them far more than they deserved, he went back to that crumbling old villa once more.

And this time he took Brita with him to give them one final offer.

"You are to move out," Brita said, in that calm way of hers that he got to watch work its magic on her family. Meaning it drove them into rages, and she knew it. She depended on it, this not entirely civilized wife of his. "The villa will be mine eventually, of course, when you are all dead." She smiled in a bloodthirsty way at her father, when she said that, making Asterion proud. Vasilis only glowered in response. "All I would need to do is wait you out, but I don't want to. I would like you all to leave, and give me the estate when you do."

"As you have already pointed out so impolitely, it will one day be yours. Why should we give you anything?" her stepmother asked icily.

"Because I will give you whatever home you wish," Asterion said then. And he did not put any parameters on that. He barely raised a brow as he watched high value real estate dance through their heads like sugarplums. "The only stipulation is that it cannot be here. The entire Martis estate, this entire part of the island, will be Brita's alone. And if you're caught here, let me be clear, you will be arrested for trespassing. Just so we understand each other."

And so it was that he rehoused the lot of his unpleasant in-laws, sending them off to whatever far-distant place they desired, and Brita was able to make her refuge a reality. She spent two solid years renovating the old villa, honoring its history, and making sure to continue to keep the staff who had always been her only friends. Or pay for the retirement they deserved if that was their preference.

When their eldest daughter was nearly three and Brita was big and round with their second child, the refuge was opened at last.

"I am a man who keeps my promises," he told her at the gala that evening, there in the villa restored to its former glory that served as the home of the wilderness foundation Brita had formed.

"Those were the easy promises," she replied airily, though her eyes gleamed. "There will be a lifetime to work on the others."

And she kissed him, there in public, the way she always did.

As if she wanted everyone else to see the wildness in him that was never too far from the surface.

As if she wanted to bring it out.

One night, years later, he came back from a business trip to find the labyrinth house shockingly empty of his wife and their children and Dimitra, who was hale and hearty and would likely live forever. She liked to spend time here with all five of her local grandchildren, the three older girls and the twin boys who'd come after, all of whom made certain that the maze of glass and steel was filled with their particular brand of joyful chaos.

Asterion barely recognized the place without them in it, making the glass and steel warm.

He showered off his work and climbed up that spiral stair that he could never use without thinking of that night. When his beloved had led him on a merry chase, then took him to an actual, literal cliff before loving him into submission.

With an arrow or two, for emphasis.

Asterion knew that he was far happier than most.

And he worked as hard as he was able to keep it so.

He wandered into the trees the way he had so many years ago. And by now there was an easy path between the house and Brita's favorite spots, so there was no need to crash about as he had that fateful night—though just like then, he caught sight of that same watchful wolf that his children liked to say watched over them at night.

Heracles had never quite taken to Asterion, but he watched over his mistress's love all the same.

He made his way over the hill to the cliffs he would always think of as theirs alone, and he stopped at the edge of the clearing as he had long ago, when he thought he was merely pretending to be besotted with this woman.

The sun was making a kind of ladder across the sea. And his wife, his goddess, the mother of his children and his eternal huntress, stood at the edge, with five little bodies pressed in all around her.

"Make room," he ordered his family as he walked to the cliff's edge and pulled his babies into his arms as they squealed in delight that he was home. "You know I don't like to miss the sunset."

He didn't like to miss a moment of this. He missed as few as he could.

Asterion would teach his children how to rule the world he'd made for them. He couldn't wait to see what they made of it.

But Brita was already teaching them how to love it.

The way she'd taught him how to love her and them and everything else that mattered.

The way he planned to do until the moon took them back.

But not anytime soon.

Not if he, Asterion Teras, had anything to say about it.

And he usually did.

* * * * *